USHIG

USHIG

Annemarie Allan

Kelpies

Kelpies is an imprint of Floris Books

First published in 2010 by Floris Books

© 2010 Annemarie Allan

The publisher acknowledges a Lottery grant
from the Scottish Arts Council towards the
publication of this series.

British Library CIP Data available

ISBN 978-086315-743-1

Printed in Great Britian
by Cromwell Press Group, Trowbridge

For my mother, Maria Clark.
A true storyteller.

Prologue

She peered round the rock, clinging tightly to its barnacled surface. The boy was still there, absorbed in a small heap of shells piled up in front of him. She frowned at the sight of that strange face, those odd eyes, like two different coloured pebbles, and the hair on his head, brown streaked with green — not a colour she had ever seen before.

He looked up for a moment and she ducked behind the rock, but another quick peek told her he had seen nothing.

With a smooth shiver of movement, she shed her skin and paddled round to where the tide lapped gently against the shore. Out of the water, free of her warm grey fur, the wind nibbled at her human flesh like a shoal of tiny fish.

"What are you doing?"

The boy glanced up. "Aren't you cold?"

Again she asked, "What are you doing?"

"Telling my fortune." He gathered the shells into his palm and threw them down on the sand. After a moment's thought, he pointed to a dark brown shell, the one lying furthest from the others.

"That one means I will travel far." He reached out and touched another. "But this one lies between me and my goal." He gave it a brief, sidelong look and flicked it away. "All the same, I will find what I seek."

She crouched beside him and placed one pale finger on two shells lying side by side, one brown, the other mottled black and white. "What are these?"

He shrugged. "One is truth and one is understanding. They lie together, so each is bound up with the other."

"Will you tell my fortune?"

He gave a sharp nod. Amusement flickered in his odd-coloured eyes as she reached out and gathered the shells to toss them in her turn.

Once again brown and black lay together, this time in a hollow in the sand. He frowned down at them. "The truth is hidden from you."

She smiled. "Do you think so?"

His lips smiled in return, but his eyes were as cold as the ocean depths.

She sat back on her heels, staring at him with a doubtful frown, then she jumped to her feet, scattering shells in every direction. He called out a farewell as she dived into the sheltering waves, but there was no response.

A slow smile spread across his face. "If I fooled the selkie," he said to himself, "then I can fool others." He picked up the shells and tossed them from hand to hand, then his odd-coloured eyes narrowed and his nose twitched. His head twisted round a little further than any human head could reach. There was something in the air, an invitation, reaching out from one world to another.

He stood up and stretched and stretched and

stretched, his body growing impossibly long, arms
and legs reshaping themselves into hoof and
fetlock, his head growing larger, longer, narrower.

Then Ushig shook his long black mane and
galloped towards the hills.

Chapter 1

Ellen draped herself over the low stone wall. Her legs were aching and her boots felt twice as heavy as they had at the start of the walk. She aimed a half-hearted finger at a scarecrow stuck in the middle of a field of barley.

"That's a tattie bogle," she said, "but it's not a tattie field."

Her brother stopped beside her. "Come on, Ellen. You promised you'd keep up."

"I *am* keeping up," she said. "Your legs are longer than mine, so I've walked a lot further than you."

"Fair point," said Davie. He mopped his sweaty forehead with a red bandana then knelt down and rummaged inside his backpack until he found his camera.

"A bogle's a sort of bad-tempered, ugly fairy," said Ellen. "But I've got a charm to keep me safe."

She reached inside her jumper and pulled out a black stone hanging on a chain round her neck. Shoving her glasses up on to her forehead, she held it up to her eye and peered through the hole in the middle. Far below, rows of houses straggled inland, all the way from the shore to the railway line, where they came to an abrupt halt. It looked as though someone had taken a ruler and drawn a straight line between town and country. From up here, the only sign of movement was a train speeding its way towards the distant sprawl that marked the outskirts of Edinburgh.

Davie took a couple of pictures of the view, then he glanced across at her. "What have you got there?"

"I told you," said Ellen, "it's a charm to keep me safe."

"Huh," Davie snorted. "That's just a bit of melted iron from the old mine. They must have seen you coming. How much did you pay for it?"

"None of your business." Ellen tucked the charm back out of sight and reached into her pocket. Pulling out a pack of wine gums she popped several into her mouth at once, then handed the pack to Davie.

"Anyway," she declared in a slightly gummy voice, "it *does* work."

"Oh yeah?" Davie slid the camera into the backpack and pulled out a scrappy piece of paper.

"Take a look around." Ellen stretched out both hands and turned in a slow circle. "I don't see any fairies. Do you?"

Davie laughed as he unfolded the paper. "Well let's just hope they don't like wine gums." He looked down at the hand-drawn map for a moment or two, then he stood up and looked around.

"This is nearly the top of Rigley Hill. That's the way to the Lammermuirs." He pointed to where the road forked off to the left.

Ellen frowned at the sight of the hills, hazy in the distance. "We're not going there!"

"Don't worry," said Davie. "We want the other road — the one that leads up Birsley Brae." He chewed on a wine gum as he studied the map. "When we get to Fa'side Castle, we turn on to a footpath then follow a track through the woods. The loch is at the end of the track." Davie stuffed the paper in his pocket, hitched the backpack on to his shoulders and handed the sweets to Ellen. "We've still got a good bit further to go."

Ellen cast a wistful glance back down the hill. "Just as long as we get to eat at the top. I'm starving!" Breakfast had been a slice of stale bread with the last scrapings of jam from the bottom of the jar.

"Well you'd better keep up then," Davie grinned at her as he moved off, "because I've got the sandwiches."

With a deep sigh, Ellen nudged her glasses on to her nose, pushed back the thick brown hair that straggled loose from her ponytail and joined her brother on the road.

Side by side, they set off on the long smooth climb, past fields of nodding barley, watching the old stone keep at the top of the hill grow slowly larger until, at last, they were standing below it.

"Just a little bit further," said Davie.

"You said we could eat at the top." Walking always made Ellen hungry.

"No I didn't." Davie pulled out the map and took another look. "We have to find the footpath that leads to the wood."

Accepting defeat, she turned and looked back the way they had come. They were much higher now. She could see right across the Firth of Forth to the start of the northern mountains, a thick smudge of grey against the blue sky.

"This way." Davie moved forward confidently and Ellen followed, grateful for the shelter of the trees on either side of the road. It was like walking through a cool, green tunnel.

Not long after, he stopped beside a gap in the wall and pointed to a little track meandering off into the trees. "This must be it."

He set off enthusiastically, clearly just as relieved as Ellen that the walk was nearly over. Ellen stepped across the broken wall, then she hesitated. For no real reason she felt oddly unwilling to follow the path.

Something about this place made the back of her neck prickle. Maybe because the air was so calm and still, almost as though the world was holding its breath. Forcing her unease to the back of her mind, she took a deep breath and followed Davie into the pine-scented twilight, where she came to an abrupt halt when something grabbed hold of her hair.

Her momentary panic dissolved when she realized it was only a thin tendril from a bramble bush, but by the time she freed herself, Davie had already disappeared round a bend in the track. She hurried to catch up, stumbling over moss-covered branches and gnarled tree roots, her feet sending up puffs of dust from the thick carpet of pine needles. This path had clearly not been used for a long time.

"Davie! Wait for me!" Her voice bounced off the

trees and faded into silence. Ellen found herself
moving faster and faster. She was almost running
by the time she rounded yet another corner and
came to a sudden halt on the edge of a little glade
filled with drifts of wild lupins. The loch they had
walked so far to find was right in front of her. She
saw Davie standing with his back to the water,
watching out for her, one hand up to shield his
eyes from the dappled sunlight.

He waved and Ellen waved back, then she walked
forward until she was waist deep in flowers. She
knelt down on the sun-warmed earth and took a
deep breath, inhaling the rich, peppery scent of the
lupins. From somewhere nearby, a bird whistled
a complicated series of notes. Ellen whistled back
and laughed in delight when the bird answered.

She took off her glasses and rubbed her eyes,
then tilted the lenses to and fro to catch the
sunlight, sending a rainbow of different colours
bouncing and sparkling across the still surface of
the water.

"That's called diffraction." Davie had his pack
on the ground and was rooting around inside it.

Ellen didn't care what it was called. She just
liked the way the broken shafts of coloured light
danced above the water.

"Well done, Ellen," said Davie. "Here's your
reward. Catch!" He tossed an apple in her direction
and bent down to pull off his boots. Tucking his
socks carefully inside the boots, he rolled up his
trousers and walked towards the little loch. After
days of dry weather, it had shrunk in on itself,
leaving a muddy rim all round the edge. Davie

squelched across the muck and then sighed with relief as his feet hit the cool water.

Ellen rolled over and stared at a ladybird crawling up a tall blade of grass. Aunt Marian had been right. This was a magical place. The bird whistled again and Ellen whistled back. This time there was no answer. She whistled again and repeated the old rhyme Aunt Marian had taught her. *"I call you once. I call you twice. I call you three times over."* In a place as beautiful as this, anything that answered her call was bound to be friendly. Sure enough, the bird began to sing again.

She sat up and bit into the apple, watching Davie make his way carefully round the edge of the water. In a minute, when her legs had stopped wobbling, she thought she might join him.

A cloud passed over the sun and the bird fell silent. Ellen felt goose bumps prickling her arms. She saw Davie reach down and pick something out of the mud.

"What's that?"

"A skull," called Davie. "A big one."

"It's probably just a sheep."

Davie was too absorbed in the thing he held in his hands to pay any attention to Ellen. She stood up and walked round the edge of the pool towards him.

"Maybe it fell in the water and couldn't get out."

"Maybe," agreed Davie. "It looks pretty deep in the middle." He lifted it up for her to see.

Ellen stared at the long, narrow skull. Drips of muddy water were running from the end of a small tuft of hair still clinging to the bone. "That's gross,

Davie!" She knocked it out of his hand. It fell back into the mud and lay there, grinning up at her.

Davie frowned. "Looks like a horse to me. Do you think we should take it back with us? People might be looking for a lost animal." He wriggled one foot and the skull rocked from side to side. Muddy water sloshed in and out of the eye sockets. "I don't suppose they'd want it back now, do you?"

"No ... let's just leave it." Ellen reached out and tugged his arm, aware of a sudden sense of urgency. "I want to go. Now."

"But we only just got here! I'm not ..." Davie stopped. He turned his head. "Did you hear that?"

Ellen listened. A breeze tugged the treetops, setting the leaves rustling. Was that the noise of branches scraping against each other? Or was it something else? The wind ruffled the surface of the loch and Ellen wrinkled her nose at the smell of stagnant water mingled with the odour of rotting plants.

She bit her lip in frustration, watching Davie pick his way slowly and carefully back to dry land. He reached for his boots and socks, then stopped and looked round again.

"There's something moving. Over there." He pointed to a dense thicket of bushes crowding down towards the pool. "It's coming this way."

He was right. The noise was much louder now. Something large was forcing its way through the bushes. Along with the cracking of branches, they could hear snorting and huffing. Ellen listened with mounting dread, unable to rid herself of the unreasonable belief that the rhyme had worked.

Something was coming — something much more dangerous than a singing bird.

"It's probably a deer," said Davie very quietly.

"Then why are you whispering?"

"Why are you?" Davie frowned. "It doesn't seem likely, though, does it? A deer would never come this close to people. They're too shy."

Ellen resisted the babyish urge to grab her brother's hand as she watched the bushes tremble. A large head emerged from the tangled undergrowth and she let go the breath she didn't know she'd been holding.

"It's just a pony!" Her voice was wobbly with relief.

The little horse whuffed and shook its head. Then, with a final effort, it forced itself free of the bushes and walked calmly towards them.

"It must have come from the riding school," said Davie, watching the pony snatch up a clump of grass. "It's not been out with anyone, though. It's got reins, but no saddle."

The pony looked at them, chewing casually with its square, slightly yellow teeth, as though its task was now complete and it was up to them to decide what happened next. Ellen stepped forward and ran her hand down the smooth velvet nose, then patted the pony tentatively on the shoulder. Its glossy coat was deep brown, almost black, and it felt slightly damp, as though the animal had been sweating. It didn't seem anxious, though. Or upset.

The pony turned away and lowered its head to the grass once more.

"We ought to let somebody know."

Davie lifted the backpack and pulled out his phone, but when he switched it on, there was no signal.

"It must be one of those dead places," he said at last.

Ellen shivered. Davie was right. This was definitely a place of the dead.

"We'll just have to head for the road," he decided. "Once we get out of the trees it should be okay. Maybe we should take the pony with us," he added as an afterthought. "Somebody must be looking for it."

The breeze picked up, tugging at Ellen's clothes, urging her to get away from this place as fast as she could. She looked up to see clouds gathering overhead. For the first time since they had arrived at Aunt Marian's the previous week, the weather was turning gloomy.

Shifting impatiently from foot to foot, she waited for Davie to dry his feet and unroll his socks. He pulled on his boots, knotting each lace with a painstaking thoroughness that set her teeth on edge. When he was finally ready to leave, she tugged on the reins, pulling the pony towards the track, but the little horse stayed exactly where it was, all four feet planted firmly on the ground.

"It doesn't want to go."

"I can see that!" Davie reached for the reins, but no matter how much he pulled and heaved and tugged, the stubborn creature refused to budge.

"Maybe you should get on its back," he said at last. "Then I can pull and you can give it a kick to get it going."

"Why me?" Ellen found herself strangely unwilling to do as her brother suggested.

"Because I'm too tall," said Davie patiently. "I'd be too heavy for it."

Ellen couldn't deny it. Since his thirteenth birthday a few months ago, Davie had been growing non-stop. Mum was buying him new clothes every few weeks. Ellen was eleven, but small for her age.

"Besides," said Davie, "you like horses."

"Why can't we just leave it here and get someone to collect it?"

It was a reasonable question, but Davie didn't seem to think so. He hated to give up on anything.

"Please, Ellen." Davie, too, now seemed gripped by an urgent desire to get away from this little glade and the deep, still pool of water at its centre. "Just do it, okay?"

But it was no use. Every time she took hold of its neck, the pony turned away, always in the same direction, so that they both moved round in a circle. When Davie tried to hold it steady, it simply stepped away from them both.

"That's it! I don't care how small you are!" Davie grabbed the reins with one hand, took hold of the pony's shaggy mane with the other and swung himself on to its back. He didn't need to jump. Ellen smiled at the sight of her brother perched on the little horse, his feet scraping the ground.

But the smile lasted barely a moment before the pony screamed and bared its teeth. It swelled up and out, no longer an amiable little creature but a huge, black horse, kicking at the air with powerful front legs, glaring at Ellen from eyes that rolled wildly in its head. Davie lost his grip on the reins and yelled out in panic as he buried both hands in the coal black mane.

The nightmare creature shifted slightly, as though testing its balance with a rider on its back, then moved forward, its hooves making soft, sucking sounds as it crossed the waterlogged soil. Ellen stared at it in bewildered disbelief and then, with sudden, dreadful clarity, she understood what this creature was and what it intended to do.

Without pausing to think, she jumped forward and grabbed the dangling reins. "No!" yelled Davie. "Don't touch it!"

But he was too late. The horse turned its red glaring eyes on Ellen, dipped its head and opened its jaws. The square yellow teeth were gone. Instead, she was looking into a mouth filled with row after row of needle-sharp fangs.

Chapter 2

Ellen jerked away from the touch of the creature's burning breath on her skin. Her feet slipped in the mud and she lost her balance, hitting the ground hard. But she did not let go of the reins.

Neither was she crushed beneath the flailing hooves. Two huge feet landed on either side of her and she hung there, gasping, as the creature tossed its head. Its eyes — one red, one coal black — looked down at her. Davie scraped his way to a more secure position while she dangled from its head, still gripping tightly to the reins, her feet scrabbling to find something solid underfoot.

"It seems you have me," said the creature. It should have been funny, a human voice issuing from those fleshy horse lips, but nobody laughed. There was a long silence.

"A talking horse," Davie said at last. "This isn't happening." He leaned sideways, trying to get one foot on the ground, but then his eyes widened in fright. He held up both hands and Ellen saw how the coarse hair of the horse's mane had wrapped itself round his wrists like handcuffs.

"I'm stuck!"

He tried for a smile, but Ellen could see what

an effort it was. Davie was frightened. And so was she.

"Come on, Davie," she pleaded. "It's easy. Just let go and slide down." There was no disguising the quaver in her voice, even though she knew it was a very bad idea to let this creature see how scared she was.

It turned its neck to look at the boy, then shifted its mad eyes back to Ellen, who now had both feet on the ground and her hands twisted round the reins.

"He is there until I choose to let him go," it said.

Ellen swallowed. Her throat was dry and she was fighting to get enough air into her lungs to speak. "What do you want from us?"

"It was you who called me," said the creature.

"I never called you," she managed at last.

"No?" The creature glanced over her shoulder to where the skull lay, half in and half out of the water, its eye sockets staring sightlessly at the sky. "This place knows death — and you invited me here."

Its gaze returned to Ellen, willing her to give up, to let go. She tried to resist, but her determination was weakened by the knowledge that the creature might be right. Perhaps that harmless little rhyme had not been so harmless after all.

It took a great effort to look away. Above her, the sky was darkening into summer evening. Where had the afternoon gone? How long had she been holding on to the reins? The thought of the woods at night set her heart pounding.

The horse's head jerked and Ellen felt the

smooth leather slip through her sweaty fingers. Her arms ached and her legs were wobbly.

"I mean you no harm." The voice was soft now. "This world is strange to me. I wonder if you might be my guide?"

If the horse was stuck just like Davie was, then it didn't seem to be very worried about it. Ellen forced herself to ignore the voice, her thoughts turning down one blind alley after another, desperately seeking some way to get them out of the woods. At last she forced herself to say the words she did not want to say.

"You can come with us. But only if you let Davie get down."

Her brother let out a high-pitched giggle. "Ellen! Why are you talking to the horse?"

She peered at Davie over the top of the horse's head. His face was running with sweat, but he was shivering so hard she could hear his teeth rattle. His eyes had an odd, wild look, like those of the creature in front of her.

The horse face stared into her own. "You look like one who keeps her word."

Ellen nodded. She plastered what she hoped was a friendly smile on her face. If this nightmare creature left them alone for even a moment then, promise or no promise, she was never coming near it again.

An idea surfaced and she felt a flicker of hope. "My brother's right," she said. "We can't possibly explain a talking horse. There's no such thing. But if you wait here, we can go and find somewhere to hide you."

The creature tilted its head to look at her. "But then you might forget all about me."

"No, I wouldn't!" She didn't need to fake the sincerity in her voice. This encounter was something she would never forget.

"In any case, there is no need to hide me."

Ellen blinked as the black shape blurred and reformed. She saw Davie stagger slightly as his feet hit the ground then she stared down at her hands, watching the reins melt away. When she looked up again, she caught her breath in surprise at the sight of another Davie behind the first one, exact in every detail, except for thin streaks of green, like slimy water weed, in his dark brown hair.

The newcomer smiled at her. Ellen fought to control a nervous snigger. She couldn't afford to give in to the panic that lurked just below the surface of her mind. Not when there was even the slightest chance of getting away.

"That's no good," she said. "You look exactly the same." She pointed to the sweatshirt. "Even the logo."

"Logo?" The creature looked down. "This is your house badge?" He ran a finger across the writing underneath. "And your motto?"

"No," said Ellen. "That says 'Nike.' It's a brand." She ignored the puzzled frown that appeared on the face in front of her. There was no time for explanations, even if she had been willing to give them. Her mind was intent on one thing only — to get herself and her brother away from this place and this unearthly creature.

"We could go home," she said, "and get you some other clothes. Then you wouldn't look so alike."

Not waiting for an answer, she bent and picked up the backpack and walked on trembling legs to where her brother stood pale and silent, his eyes vacant.

"Come on, Davie" she said. "It's time to go."

"Clothes can be changed," said the shapeshifter. He ran a hand down his front. The logo melted away and the colour of the sweatshirt darkened from grey to black. "And so can the face I wear."

Ellen saw the nose grow a little longer and the cheekbones sharpen, until it was no longer an identical copy of her brother's.

She made one last effort. "But why do you want to come with us?"

The creature shrugged, a human gesture that took Ellen by surprise. "It is lonely here," he said. "The wild places are almost gone. I would like to see the world your folk have made."

It seemed so reasonable, but only if you forgot the look in the creature's eye when Davie had been trapped on its back. Ellen bit her lip, trying to think. There was no real choice. The only way to find help was to take the boy-thing along with them.

She glanced at Davie, hoping he would take over the way he usually did, but her brother didn't even look at her. His eyes were vague and unfocused, as though his mind was elsewhere.

"Let's go, Davie," she said at last, giving him a push in the direction of the path. He stumbled forward obediently and Ellen followed, shivering a little at the thought of the creature that walked so close behind.

The woods were darker now, and not just because of the clouds gathering in the evening sky. Somehow, the trees crowded closer to the path than before. Bramble bushes reached out with thorny branches to snag their hair and clothes, almost as though they were unwilling to let them pass.

By the time they emerged from the tunnel of trees, a gentle pattering of raindrops warned of bad weather to come, but the boy who was not a boy didn't seem to mind the weather. He walked out of the wood, his eyes sparkling with interest as he spotted the huge pylons marching across the fields towards the distant hills. Even the tarmac surface beneath their feet attracted his eager look.

In silence, they carried on, past the looming bulk of Fa'side Castle and down the slope. When they arrived at the place where Ellen had stopped for a rest, she saw the creature nod in the direction of the scarecrow and was almost sure she saw the scarecrow dip its head in reply.

The false boy paused to examine a burnt-out car lying half on the road and half on the verge. Davie stopped walking. He let loose a great shuddering breath and turned to Ellen. She looked anxiously into his face.

"We never had our picnic," he said.

Ellen smiled in relief. The blank look was gone from her brother's eyes. "It doesn't matter," she said. "It's raining now anyway. Let's just go home."

He nodded his agreement. "That was quite a

walk," he said. "And you're right — your legs are shorter than mine. Still ..." he added cheerfully, "at least it's downhill all the way back." His gaze shifted and Ellen saw him raise his eyebrows in surprise as though he noticed the other boy for the first time.

The creature looked up and their eyes met. After a long moment, Davie looked back at his sister and Ellen frowned. The vagueness was back.

Davie blinked, then he turned to look behind them. "Where's the pony? I thought we were bringing it with us."

"Davie," she said urgently, ignoring the chilly raindrops that plastered her hair to her head and ran down her back inside her clothes. "Don't you remember? You found the skull — and then you climbed on to the pony."

Her brother's eyes flicked away.

"You do remember!" she insisted. But she didn't have time to argue. There was something else on her mind. She lowered her voice. "Davie, we mustn't invite it into the house. They can't come in unless they're invited."

Davie looked from her to the boy. "Why are you calling him 'it'?"

"I think it's one of the Peerie Folk," she whispered back, glancing sideways at the creature, now poking warily at the rusting hulk with a stick. "It's a kelpie — a water wraith."

Davie laughed. "Right," he said. "It's a water wraith! There's a lot of them about."

Ellen flinched at the scorn in his voice. But Davie hadn't finished.

"You've been banging on about fairies ever since you got that book from Aunt Marian. And now, when you think you've found one, all you care about is not inviting it into the house!"

He was talking about her birthday present from last summer. The book had belonged to her grandmother, her mother's mother, who had died long ago.

Ellen tried to fight back, but her heart wasn't in it. "You're just jealous she didn't give it to you."

"You wish!"

Davie was right. Ellen was deeply disappointed when she unwrapped the shiny new paper to find an ancient dog-eared book written by a man called Robert Kirk. The author claimed he had been stolen away by what he called the "Peerie Folk" when he was a small child. It was only because Aunt Marian was watching that she opened the book and read the first sentence.

"The shadow woman who brought food and drink was nothing to me — not until the moment she ripped the veil of confusion from my eyes."

It was interesting enough that Ellen picked up the book again later that evening. Once she began to read, she couldn't put it down. All last winter, she had followed Robert Kirk on his journey across the land of the Peerie Folk, through a world of mysterious, magical creatures: some merely odd, others terrifying, but each one utterly real.

"Listen to me, Davie," insisted Ellen, determined to make her point. "They don't belong here. They have to be invited."

"Well, you *did* invite him, didn't you? You said he could come with us."

She stared at him. It seemed that he did remember some things after all. Stubbornly, she insisted, "I didn't invite *it* in the house."

He rolled his eyes and turned away. "You can stop nagging," he said. "I won't be asking him to stay."

Ellen swallowed her hurt and annoyance. It wasn't Davie's fault. He didn't really mean to be horrible. It wasn't like him at all. He was still wobbly from shock.

The water wraith threw away the stick and walked back to join them. "Who destroyed it?" He nodded towards the car.

Davie shrugged. "Joyriders, I suppose."

"Joyriders?" The creature rolled the word around in his mouth, then favoured them with a sharp look. "Do you belong to these Joyriders?"

Davie laughed. "No," he said. "We're just ordinary kids. My name's Davie and this is my little sister Ellen."

Ellen jabbed her glasses further up her nose, wishing Davie hadn't been so quick to establish how harmless they were.

"Davie and Ellen." The creature looked from one to the other and licked his lips as though he had just swallowed a delicious little morsel. "I am Ushig."

His eyes focused on Ellen and she jerked back as his finger jabbed at her face. The nails were thick and horny, like stubby claws.

"What is that?"

"Glasses," said Davie cheerfully. "She can't see properly without them."

Ellen turned away and trudged on through the rain. Davie shouldn't have given the creature their names. Her book said names could be used to keep you in their power. And right now it was Davie, not her, who couldn't see properly. This wasn't a boy ... and Ushig wasn't his name. It was just another word for a water wraith.

She risked a glance in the creature's direction. He smiled. Opening his palm to reveal a handful of coloured shells, he tossed them into the air, then reached out and caught them all without dropping a single one.

Chapter 3

The country road ended at the railway line. As they headed along the platform towards the bridge, Ellen caught sight of an express train rushing towards them and automatically reached out to pull Ushig behind the yellow line. She let go almost immediately. His clothes felt like skin, not fabric.

Ushig staggered backwards as the train sped past in a sudden furious explosion of noise and air. In the silence that followed, he looked hard at Ellen, then gave a sharp nod.

"I thank you." His mouth set in a narrow line, he watched the train disappear down the track. "There were human folk in the belly of that beast."

Davie flicked his eyes from Ushig to Ellen, then he gave an exaggerated sigh. "Right," he said, clearly under the impression this was some sort of game. "It's a monster that eats people. And I thought it was just a machine that took you where you wanted to go."

Ellen followed Davie and Ushig up the steps and over the bridge, her mind still casting about for some way to unglue themselves from the water wraith. She looked hopefully up and down, but both platforms were deserted. There was no one here to help them and in any case, what could she

say that might sound believable? She remembered
the stick Ushig had used to poke the burnt-out car.
Magical creatures were supposed to dislike cold
iron. But her brief hope flickered and died when
she watched Ushig cross the iron bridge without
any apparent discomfort.

Walking into Aldhammer was like travelling
backwards through time. First came the curvy
roads and red brick houses of the new estate,
each with a garage to one side; then the miners'
cottages, with big front gardens, wooden doors
and a single window on each side, like something
from a child's drawing. If they walked on they
would reach the narrow winding lanes leading
down to the sea, but they weren't going that far
today. Aunt Marian lived in one of the miners'
cottages.

Ushig's eyes were everywhere. He gazed in
puzzled interest at the pavements and houses,
laughed in delight as a group of brightly coloured
cyclists swished past along the rainswept road and
frowned at the car that almost hit him when he
stepped off the pavement. Ellen felt her cheeks
grow hot with embarrassment when he stopped in
front of a woman laden with bags of shopping and
eyed her up and down before he stepped aside to
let her pass.

"Where are they all going?"

"I don't know," said Ellen. "Home? Work? To
the shops, maybe."

A man strolled by with a portly black labrador.
The dog swung its head towards Ushig and let
loose a deep menacing growl. Ushig growled back.

The dog instantly dropped its eyes and sidled closer to its master with its tail between its legs.

"Davie," Ellen hissed urgently as they rounded the final corner and Aunt Marian's house came into view. "Don't let it in the house. Please."

Davie reached out and patted her arm in a reassuring gesture. Ellen wanted to growl at him the way the dog had growled at Ushig.

Aunt Marian's cat, Bill, was in his usual spot in the rowan tree beside the gate. He lay stretched out along a branch with his head on his paws and his back legs hanging down on either side. He looked as if he was sleeping, but Ellen could see his tail twitch as raindrops dripped through the leaves and on to his back.

Ushig's eyes flicked towards the tree and Ellen remembered that rowan was supposed to be another protection. Hoping it worked better than iron, she opened the gate and shut it again as soon as Davie followed her inside.

"We have to go in now," she said firmly.

"If you must," said Ushig.

Bill opened one eye, then he leapt out the tree, all his fur standing on end until he was twice his normal size. With a horrendous yowl, he raced up the path, his belly close to the ground and his tail spread out like a bottlebrush. When Ellen and Davie reached the door, the cat flap was swinging to and fro, but Bill himself was nowhere to be seen.

She glanced back while Davie fumbled in his pocket for the key. Ushig was watching them from the pavement. He smiled at her and she frowned, wondering why he seemed so content to let them go.

At last Davie got the door open and they tumbled inside, heading for the comforting familiarity of Marian's cluttered kitchen. They sat down at the table and stared at each other.

"Where's Aunt Marian?" Ellen said at last. "She said she'd be home."

"That doesn't mean much," said Davie. Ellen nodded, thinking of the nail-biting wait when they stepped off the train in Edinburgh. Nobody had come to meet them. It was almost fifteen minutes later when they saw Aunt Marian rushing towards them, a look of apology on her flustered face.

All the same, Ellen enjoyed spending time with Aunt Marian, even if she was a bit scatty. She liked wandering around the ruined harbour, helping to collect the plants and seaweeds her aunt used to make her dyes, peering into rock pools in search of whelks and prawns and anemones, while Davie explored further afield.

Ellen watched him across the table, wishing that she hadn't nagged to go with him on today's expedition. But then, if she hadn't gone, he might never have come home again. She shivered at the thought.

Davie leaned on the table with his head in his hands. "I feel woozy," he said. "It must be hunger. We never ate much of that picnic." He delved into the backpack, took out his camera and upended the rest of the contents on to the table.

Ellen stared at the squashed crisps, the bruised apples and the cartons of juice. "It's not hunger," she said. "It's Ushig." She looked hard at her brother, willing him to listen. "He's a kelpie. A water wraith. He took the shape of a horse so you would climb on his back. He wanted to drown you, Davie."

Ellen's fingers crept towards the chain round her neck. The charm was worth something after all if it had stopped Ushig from taking her brother.

Davie made a face and opened his mouth to argue, but the sound of the gate unlatching and closing stopped any further conversation. Ellen jumped to her feet and hurried to the living room window, peering out past the explosion of damp grass and wild flowers that was her aunt's front garden. "It's Aunt Marian," she called. She turned back to the window. Ushig was no longer beside the gate. "I think he's gone."

Davie's voice spoke in her ear. "No, he's not."

Ellen followed his pointing finger across the neatly gravelled expanse of next door's garden and her heart gave a little lurch. Davie was right. Ushig was talking to old Mrs Fraser. He held out his hand. Mrs Fraser bent to look, then she shook her head and turned away.

Marian kicked open the front door and staggered through to the kitchen with a wicker basket in one hand and a carrier bag in the other, both dripping and smelling strongly of the sea.

"Sorry," she said when Ellen appeared in the doorway. "I didn't expect you back so soon. The tide was out and I took a walk along the shore. Just give me a minute to get this lot into my workshop."

"Don't you want to hear about our walk?" Ellen was desperate for the reassurance of some adult company.

But Marian was already halfway out the door, heading for the shed where she worked on her fabrics and her dyes. From the dreamy look on her face, it would be a while before she surfaced again.

Ellen went back to the living room. Davie was lounging in a chair, flicking from one TV channel to another. She peered out the window again. The rain had cleared. Puddles glinted in the evening sunlight. Ushig was wandering up and down the street, examining the houses with great interest. He looked like a tourist.

"Do you think he can change into anything he wants?"

Davie snorted. "Are you still convinced he changed from a horse into a boy?" He flicked off the television and turned to look at her, a gleam of mischief in his eye. "So ... he changes into things that carry people? Like a bicycle? Don't you think people would notice a bicycle speeding towards the nearest stretch of deep water?"

"It's not funny." Ellen frowned. "Don't you remember what happened at the loch?"

"Of course I do," said Davie. "We went for a walk and found a pony. We couldn't move the blasted thing out of the woods. Then that creepy boy turned up and followed us home." It was his turn to frown. "You can't let your imagination take over your whole life, you know."

"I give up," snapped Ellen. She headed for the front door, not because she wanted to go anywhere near the thing lurking outside, but because she couldn't bear the thought of sitting in here wondering what Ushig was up to.

"Make sure you stay in the street," Davie called after her. "Don't go wandering off with that boy."

Ellen stepped outside, knowing that if Davie had seen what she had seen, those rows of pointed teeth and the mad, glaring eyes, he would never have let her out the door.

She stopped at the gate and watched Ushig walk towards her, feeling a little reassured when she saw how he avoided coming too close to the rowan tree.

He nodded at Mrs Fraser's front door. "I offered to tell her fortune," he said. "She told me she had sponsored enough already."

Ellen wasn't interested in explaining. She wanted explanations of her own. "What do you want from us?"

Ushig's eyes held a glint of amusement, as though he saw a joke he didn't want to share. "I mean you no harm."

She glared at him. Did he think she was stupid?

He pointed to the sky. "What's that?"

She looked up. "It's the sun."

"The sun?" He gazed at it in wonder and delight. "In our world, light is the gift of the Lady."

"What lady?"

Ushig didn't answer. He bent his head to look at the gutter, where a mixture of oil, rain and watery sunshine had combined to form a glistening, iridescent puddle.

"That's a fallen rainbow," she said, and felt a wicked sense of satisfaction when he nodded in apparent understanding. Her delight evaporated when he looked up at her and snapped, "Why is Davie not with you?"

"He's staying indoors," she said.

Ushig took a step closer. "You offered me your company. A promise freely given cannot be recalled."

"It wasn't freely given," she said. "And anyway, it'll be dark soon. We won't be coming out again tonight."

There was a long pause while he stared hard at her, as though he wanted to see right inside to the thoughts in her head. At last he gave a nod. "After darkness comes the light. Until tomorrow then."

Ellen watched him walk slowly away up the middle of the road, then she turned and headed back inside. With any luck, before tomorrow, he would come face to face with an absolutely enormous truck.

She found Davie in the kitchen, staring into the fridge. "There's no butter. Should I make some cheese on toast?" He looked doubtfully at the hard lump of cheese in his hand. "Do you think these are tooth marks?"

Ellen shrugged. Davie sighed and put the cheese back.

"Let's have some soup. It should be okay. It's out of a can."

Ellen pushed the bag and the rest of the litter to one side of the table and fetched bowls and spoons. "He says he wants to explore." She sat down and wrinkled her nose thoughtfully. "But I don't trust him."

Davie sat down opposite, looking at his little sister as though she had grown an extra head.

"He's just a weird kid," he said. "Don't let it bother you."

"I'm telling you, Davie," she insisted. "He wants something."

"Maybe he does," said Davie. He sat down and attacked the first food he'd had for hours. "Anyway, you were right not to let him in the house."

Ellen raised her eyebrows at this admission, but she was generous enough not to crow.

They both froze as the back door opened, but it was only Marian. "Great!" she said, as she spotted the soup. "I'm starving." She found herself a spoon and lifted the pot off the stove. The sound of metal scraping against metal set Ellen's teeth on edge.

"Who was that lad hanging around outside when I came in? I haven't seen him before." For once the vagueness was gone. She was looking directly at Davie.

"He's just a kid from the new estate." Davie shot a warning glance at Ellen.

Ellen had no intention of leaving it at that, even though she was sure she was about to make a real fool of herself. "He's not ..."

She got no further before Davie interrupted. "He's not local. He's a visitor. He was looking for a house near here."

"What house?"

Ellen opened her mouth, but once again Davie got there first. "Don't know, really," he said. "Anyway, he's gone now."

Marian nodded, then she glanced at her watch and dumped the pot and spoon in the sink.

"Sorry," she said. "Must get back. I'm timing my colours." She turned in the doorway. "Tomorrow, I'll make pizza. It's your last night, after all." She smiled at Davie. "Feeling nervous?"

Davie frowned. "Why should I be nervous?"

"Well," said Marian, "it's your first time travelling back without a grown-up."

Davie's frown deepened. "We made it up here without any trouble."

"I know. I'm sure you'll be fine." Marian sighed. "I suppose I'll hardly see Laura any more, now she's letting you two travel on your own." She looked at her watch again and made for the door.

"You could always come and stay with us," Ellen said.

"Oh, Ellen." Marian stopped with one hand on the doorknob. "I couldn't! The tube — the traffic — everything so noisy and dirty!"

"Might be worth it to see your sister, though," said Davie.

It was Marian's turn to frown. "I love my sister, Davie, but you know I don't like London — and Laura doesn't like the sea."

This was something that had always puzzled Ellen. "How can you grow up beside the sea and not want to see it ever again?"

"That's a question you should ask your mother, not me," said Marian firmly. "She has her reasons. Now I really have to go or I'll lose a whole week's work."

Marian smiled in their general direction and then she was gone, oblivious to the grim look they exchanged behind her back.

"What was that all about?" Ellen asked her brother.

Davie shrugged. "Who knows? You'll have to do what Aunt Marian said and ask Mum." His face brightened. "Looks like we might get a decent tea tomorrow though."

"Pizza!" grumbled Ellen. "Burnt crust, more like."

Davie smiled. "Better not let Aunt Marian hear you say that."

She dipped her spoon in the bowl and flicked the last of the soup in his direction. Davie laughed and flicked some back.

Chapter 4

Blood-red eyes glimmered in the darkness of the night. Frozen with fear, Ellen watched the shadow creature slowly but surely close the gap between them.

"Wake up!" She screamed the words inside her head, unable to get her lips to move or force the air out of her strangled throat. But only when she felt the touch of burning breath on her cheek did terror lend her the strength to fight her way back into the real world.

She lay in bed, her heart pounding, grateful for the faint breeze from the open window on her hot and sweaty face. After a while she threw back the covers and grabbed her clothes. She cast an envious glance at the top of her brother's head, the only part of him that showed above the duvet. Davie didn't seem to be having any trouble sleeping. In the bathroom she splashed cold water on her face, pulled on her clothes and dragged a comb through her tangled hair.

Marian was already in the kitchen, hunched over a cup of coffee. She smiled at Ellen. "Ready for a walk?"

Ellen would much rather have crawled back into bed, but she didn't want to disappoint her aunt. This was the last day of the holiday. Tomorrow, they would be heading home. After a quick cup of tea she followed Aunt Marian out of the house, feeling as though someone had sandpapered the inside of her head.

All the way down to the sea, her eyes darted nervously from one side of the lane to the other, but she saw no sign of Ushig. Her mood lifted a little. Maybe he had found more interesting things to do than follow them around. And Davie was indoors. Ushig couldn't get at him there.

Aunt Marian stopped at a rock pool to scrape something green and slimy into a plastic bag, while Ellen walked down to the water's edge. She watched the foam hiss and bubble over the shingle. This time tomorrow, she would be heading back to her own life and her own friends, but she knew she would miss the sea.

She picked up a handful of flat stones and sent them skimming across the waves. It would be such a relief to tell Aunt Marian everything. It was a happy thought, but all the same that was impossible. Marian might be vague and dreamy, but she was still a grown-up. She would think Ellen was crazy, especially if Davie didn't back her up. And Davie seemed to have convinced himself that Ellen was making things up.

Behind her, she heard the crunch of feet on shingle. "Look!" Marian pointed over Ellen's shoulder. "A seal!"

Out beyond the rocks, a round grey head bobbed up and down in the swell. She turned to Aunt Marian with a smile of delight and caught an odd, guarded look in her aunt's eye. When she looked again, the seal was staring back at her. It disappeared with a suddenness that made her blink, but moments later it popped up again, even closer to the shore.

Ellen felt the tension slip away as she watched the whiskery face peer at her from between the waves. She let out a deep sigh as it sank once more beneath the water. "I've never seen a seal out there before!"

"They've always been there," said Aunt Marian, "but they're a bit shy. Are you ready to go back to the house yet?"

"I'll be up soon." Ellen was hoping the seal would come back. She drifted towards the rocks, climbed a barnacle-crusted slab and looked out over the water, then moved forward cautiously over the slippery surface, pausing to poke around in the tide pools, slithering over patches of green slime and clumps of seaweed until she reached a deep crack in the rock. Turning her back to the water she climbed down inside, landing with a crunch on a patch of damp shingle. Bare rock reared up on either side of her. It was dim and peaceful, a good place to think.

Ellen rubbed her smeary glasses on her t-shirt, put them back on and sank down with her back against the cold stone, listening to the sound of the sea scraping against the shingle. Ushig wanted something, she was sure of that, and whatever his plans were, somehow they involved her and Davie ... especially Davie.

Seized by the sudden feeling that she had left her brother alone for too long, she jumped to her feet, her fingers already scrabbling for handholds in the stone when a movement in the shadows caught her eye. She let go and peered into the darkness.

"Who's there?"

Her trembling whisper bounced off the rocks and echoed around the narrow space. She let a hand creep up to the comforting lump of the charm round her neck. It was nothing. Only a clump of seaweed flapping in the wind.

But it wasn't seaweed. Ellen caught her breath as a girl emerged from the shadows. She was taller than Ellen and looked older. Her loose, sleeveless tunic was far too thick and heavy for a summer day. The girl ran her hands over her mop of short dark hair, then lowered her arms and looked down at her fingers.

Ellen stared at them too. They were webbed. She looked up and saw the girl watching her, a wary look in her deep brown eyes. Her round face looked made for laughter, but right now it was twisted in a nervous frown. It was a face Ellen recognised. This girl had stepped right out of the pages of Robert Kirk's book.

Ellen smiled. The girl didn't smile back, but she did move a little closer.

"That one needs watching," she said.

"Who?" But Ellen didn't really need to ask. She knew who they were talking about.

"He thought I did not know him before," said the girl. "But I did." Her eyes narrowed. "What has he done?"

Ellen felt a wave of relief wash over her. This was someone who understood.

"He tried to drown my brother Davie, but I stopped him. With this, I think." She pulled out the chain and held out the stone.

The girl leaned forward and sniffed it. Ellen stifled a giggle.

"That is protection," she agreed. "But I do not think it has much power. And now that Ushig has your brother in his eye, you will need more than that." She looked into Ellen's face. "I was sent to tell you. Bridle the wraith — then he will be yours."

"But he wore a bridle yesterday," said Ellen. "It didn't stop him."

"No," said the girl, her voice sharp. "You must make one for yourself. Make it with your own hands and think of him as you weave. Bridle the water wraith and he cannot harm you."

Ellen stepped forward. "What does Ushig want with my brother?" She had so many questions she wanted to ask. Was this girl really one of those that Robert Kirk called "the folk of land and sea"? How did she know about Ushig? And why did she come here to warn her, even though the land was clearly such a fearful place for her to be?

The girl stepped back towards the dim recesses of the rock. "I do not know what he wants," she answered, "but it will be nothing good." She moved her head from side to side, as though testing the air, then she turned and slipped away.

"Wait!" Ellen reached out a hand, but it was too late. She peered at the rock, wondering how the girl had managed to squeeze through a space that was too small even for her, but there was nothing to see. And the sound of waves slapping against the rocks warned her she could not afford to linger.

Carefully, she clambered slowly out of the cleft in the rock. "A selkie," she breathed, overcome with wonder. "I saw a selkie." She had met another of the Peerie Folk and, this time, she had not been afraid. With a pang of regret she realized that the selkie had been afraid of *her*.

The sense of wonder stayed with her all the way up the narrow streets until she rounded the last corner and saw two boys crouched beside Marian's gate, intent on something lying on the pavement between them.

Davie looked up. "Hi Ellen," he said, his eyes glittering with excitement. He waved a hand at the scatter of shells on the paving stones. "Ushig's telling my fortune."

Ellen blinked. Davie was staring down at the collection of shells with an intensity that made her bite her lip.

"He says I'm going on a journey," said Davie. "But I won't be going alone — and something is waiting for me at the end." He winked at his sister. "Right now, though, he says my understanding is under a cloud."

Ellen looked from Davie to Ushig. "I think he's right."

Ushig stared up at her as Davie stood and brushed the dust off his jeans.

"Come on, then." He pushed open the gate. "We'd better go and get organized if we're going on a journey."

Ushig rose to his feet without taking his eyes

off Ellen. "You did not tell me the darkness would last so long." He scowled, his words dropping softly into the space between them. "There was a promise made. It is a dangerous thing to break a promise."

With one last malevolent glare in her direction, Ushig turned away. Ellen stared after him, her whole body trembling like a leaf in the wind.

"Ellen!"

She looked round to see Aunt Marian beckoning her indoors. Slowly, she followed her brother up the path.

"I thought you could get packed early," said Aunt Marian when Ellen arrived on the doorstep. "And then this afternoon you can help me to do some tidying up."

"But why?" Ellen couldn't understand the rush. "We've got all night to pack."

Marian wasn't listening. She was staring into the street, watching Ushig wandering down the road.

Davie directed a puzzled look at Ellen. It wasn't like Aunt Marian to be in such a hurry to get rid of them. Ellen shrugged and followed her brother and her aunt indoors. She was beginning to suspect that Aunt Marian knew more than she was prepared to admit.

Chapter 5

"Why the big rush?" Yawning, Davie watched his sister struggle out the front door next morning with both backpacks. "We haven't had breakfast yet."

Ellen didn't bother to tell him she hadn't even taken the time to brush her teeth. She threw both bags into the back of her aunt's smelly, ramshackle little car and headed back up the path to fetch the suitcase. A whiff or two of decaying seaweed was a small price to pay for a quick getaway.

"What on earth is wrong with Aunt Marian?" hissed Davie, as he was dragged unceremoniously away from a half-finished cup of tea and bundled into the back of the car.

Ellen didn't answer. She was simply grateful that, for once, her aunt was determined to arrive early at the station. Somehow she could not rid herself of the feeling that somewhere nearby lurked a creature with odd-coloured eyes, just waiting to pounce, like a cat on a mouse.

Ellen only started to relax after the car coughed and grumbled, then finally decided today was a good day for a trip. Her mood brightened as they whizzed along the city bypass and arrived at the station with plenty of time to spare.

"Just as well your Mum's picking you up," Marian said breathlessly as she hauled the bags into the train and dumped them in the luggage rack. "The tube would be impossible with this lot." She frowned at the sight of people spreading their belongings optimistically across the tables.

"Don't worry," said Davie. "We can take care of ourselves." He looked down at the tickets in his hand. "We're down that way," he said to Ellen and after a brief peck on the cheek from Marian he set off to claim their seats.

Giddy with relief now that Aldhammer was behind them, Ellen leaned out the open doorway and hugged her aunt. She let go and blinked in surprise to see Marian shoot a nervous glance at a boy standing alone on the platform. It couldn't be Ushig. Ellen knew that. He couldn't have followed them all the way to Edinburgh. After all, two days ago, he didn't even know what a train *was*.

"Take this." Marian pushed a small bunch of rowan twigs tied with red thread into Ellen's hands.

Ellen looked down at the twigs. She remembered them from her book — and the rhyme that went with them. She looked back at her aunt in sudden comprehension.

"You know, don't you?"

Marian looked back, her eyes sombre. "I don't know *what* I know, Ellen. I just think it's better to be safe than sorry."

She folded Ellen's hands around the twigs. "Laura will be angry with me about this. When I gave you the book she told me I was filling your head with nonsense." She stood on tiptoe and planted a kiss on the top of Ellen's head. "She's probably right. I'm just being silly, really."

"No! You're not!" Ellen stepped off the train and grabbed Marian's arm. "You have to talk to Davie. He won't listen to me!"

It was too late. The door alarm began to bleep and Marian stepped back. "Just try to forget all about it, Ellen. You'd better go now. You're making Davie nervous."

Reluctantly, Ellen climbed aboard the train. Her aunt smiled up at her.

"You'll be all right now. Take care of Davie ... and keep in touch."

"I will." The heavy door slid shut, bringing with it a sudden sense of relief. Marian was right. It was over now.

The train gathered speed as it left the station, flashing past roads and houses and on into open country. When it reached the coast, Ellen stared out of the window at the steep cliffs and rocky inlets, storing up pictures in her head.

Her sightseeing was interrupted by the guard arriving to check their tickets. Davie sat up straight, trying to look older than he was.

"Someone meeting you, are they?"

"Yes."

"Our mum," said Ellen, at the same time.

Davie frowned at his sister and Ellen saw the woman opposite hide a smile behind her magazine.

Not long after that they crossed the high bridge at Berwick on Tweed, where the river widened into the sea. Ellen made her usual unsuccessful attempt to catch a glimpse of Holy Island, then she settled back in her seat and opened a book.

Eventually she leaned over to Davie. "Why were you hanging around with that boy yesterday? I thought you said he was creepy."

Davie looked up from his Nintendo. "He was all right once you got to know him. I told him what you said — about him being a horse. He thought it was really funny." He leaned back in his seat and raised his eyebrows at Ellen. "Don't you think you're getting a bit old for your fairy obsession? Or are you still looking for them everywhere?"

Ellen glanced uneasily at the woman opposite and saw her hide another smile. She was glad now that she hadn't told Davie about her encounter with the seal girl yesterday morning.

Davie leaned forward and lowered his voice. "They're everywhere, aren't they?" He rolled his eyes meaningfully towards a little girl in the seat across the aisle. She had her tongue stuck in the corner of her mouth, concentrating hard on colouring in a picture of a teddy bear.

Ellen stared at her brother in surprise. This wasn't like Davie at all. "Why are you being so mean?"

Davie laughed, his eyes gleaming with that odd sparkle she had noticed lately. "It's just a joke, Ellen."

She stood up. "I'm going to the buffet. I'm hungry."

"I'd better come too," he said. "Mum said we should stay together."

Ellen wobbled her way down the train, stopping to wait for a large man to shift sideways and let her pass. He frowned up at her as though it was her fault there wasn't enough room.

Davie tapped her on the shoulder and wiggled his eyebrows meaningfully in the man's direction. "Maybe that's him," he whispered.

Ellen sighed. Ushig wasn't on the train. Davie was just winding her up. It looked as though it was going to be a very long journey.

Four hours later, they embraced the chaos of London once again, joining the crowd of passengers struggling off the train with their luggage. They fought their way down the platform against the stream of people moving in the opposite direction, eyes searching for those they had come to meet, until Davie stopped beside a pillar and dropped the suitcase with a sigh of relief. "We'll just wait here."

Ellen nodded. Mum wouldn't be far away. She was the complete opposite of her vague, dreamy sister. Moments later, she spotted her mother struggling towards them with an empty trolley.

"Trust Mum to get a trolley first!" Davie said.

"We'd better hurry. I'm parked in the drop-off zone." Mum enveloped both of them in a single hug. "Your dad's at home cooking a welcome back meal."

Half an hour later they drew up outside the house. Leaving Davie to deal with the suitcase, Ellen dashed indoors, exchanged a quick hug with her father and headed upstairs to her unnaturally tidy bedroom, where she dropped the backpack and fell back on her neatly made bed with a sigh of relief. For once, her mother's urge to straighten things up didn't annoy her. It was comforting to be back in a house where meals and clean laundry appeared without the slightest effort on her part.

All the same, she felt sad about leaving Aldhammer. She always did. Aunt Marian said the sea was in her blood and Ellen thought she must be right. This time, though, her sadness was mixed with relief.

Reaching over to her bookshelf, she pulled a well-thumbed volume on to her knee. The cloth on the cover must have been thick once, almost furry, but now it was shiny with age, its colour faded to a dusky pink. She opened it gently and ran her fingers across the words inside. *A Journey through the Invisible World*, by Robert Kirk.

In spite of its dangers, Robert Kirk did find his way across the land of the Peerie Folk. His journey ended when he reached the sea — and so did the book. There was no explanation of how he returned to his own world, his family and his home, but he must have done, otherwise the book would not be here in her hands. If it was real, of course.

Ellen lifted her head and stared out of the window. She was beginning to think that the book might not be fantasy after all. Her eyes drifted back to the title page. At the bottom was the date, 1907. Over a hundred years ago.

She flicked through the pages and stopped at a drawing of a huge black horse standing on the edge of a dark moorland loch. A desolate landscape stretched away on either side, rising slowly towards jagged mountain peaks. Facing the horse, with his back to her, stood a barefoot boy dressed in rags. He was about Davie's age. Her eyes slid down to the words below. She had read it so often she knew it almost by heart.

"The water wraith, or kelpie, is the worst kind of creature. He will trick people on to his back then take them under the water. There he will eat them. He eats everything, except the liver."

Ellen closed the book, goose bumps creeping up her arms. After a moment she opened it again, this time at her favourite picture of a woman sitting on a rock beside the sea, her naked body partly covered by her long brown hair and the thick animal pelt slung round her shoulders. She was looking straight at Ellen, her eyes wide, as though surprised by the world beyond the picture.

Ellen pulled her hair free of its ponytail and examined it thoughtfully. It was the same glossy brown as the hair on the woman in the picture — and the girl on the shore.

She sighed as she shut the book again. Leaving Ushig behind meant leaving the selkie girl as well. But she had no choice, not if that was the price she had to pay to escape the creature that had tried to drown her brother.

She laid the book on the bed and wandered over to the window. With one finger she nudged the crystal teardrop that hung there. It caught the sunlight and sent a flurry of rainbow colours dancing over the walls. Davie had talked about that at the loch, just before all this began. What was it called again? Refraction?

Shouts of laughter came from next door, followed

by the yapping of a happy dog. Her friend Rose was in the garden entertaining her two little brothers. The laughter gave way to a howl of fury from the youngest child and Ellen smiled. Ushig was far away. Everything was back to normal and that was enough for now.

"Wind's up," Dad said. "How about taking the kite over the marsh?"

"No, Dad," groaned Ellen. "I'm too full to move."

Davie was beside her, stretched out on the sofa with his feet parked on the low table in front of him, the TV remote in his hand. He rolled his eyes at Ellen. They had eaten far too much at dinner, trying to make up for a week with Aunt Marian.

They both knew that the only reason Dad wanted their company was because he needed help to get the kite in the air. While he kept his eye on the kite, Davie and Ellen would be left to smile apologetically at irritated passers-by when the black, delta-winged monster swooped dangerously low over their heads, frightening dogs and children.

"Come on!" Dad swiped Davie's feet off the table. "It'll do you both good after all that time on the train."

"Leave them alone, Mick," said Mum. "They've had a long day."

"Okay. I'll come with you."

Surprised, Ellen turned to look at her brother as he struggled to his feet.

"After that dinner, he deserves a bit of help," said Davie.

Ellen shrugged and snuggled deeper into the cushions, feeling deliciously warm and a little sleepy. Davie could go with Dad. She was more than happy to stay exactly where she was.

An hour later, they were back, their laughter echoing down the hall even before they burst into the living room. Mum exchanged a puzzled glance with Ellen.

"Hi there," she said. "Did you have a good time?"

"Great!" Dad slapped Davie on the back. "Just as well we met that friend of yours though. I thought we were going to lose the kite in the canal."

Davie was grinning from ear to ear until he saw Ellen watching and sobered up.

"What friend?" Mum wasn't really listening. The washing machine was coming to the end of its spin and she was trying to decide whether she could manage another load before bedtime.

"Nobody," Davie mumbled. "Just someone from school." He gave Ellen an odd look, then turned and left the room. She heard his feet thunder on the stairs and the sound of his bedroom door open and close. She frowned. Something about that sparkly look in Davie's eyes had set alarm bells ringing.

With a sinking heart, she stood up and followed Davie out of the room. Upstairs, in her bedroom, she opened her bag and looked down at the little bunch of rowan twigs. Carefully, she lifted them out. Then she picked up her book. Each chapter began with a rhyme. She flicked through the pages until she found the one she wanted. She stared down at the page, memorizing the words. It was important to get it exactly right.

Summoning every shred of determination she possessed, Ellen went back downstairs and pulled open the front door. Ellen paused in the doorway, wishing desperately that she could just climb into bed and pull the covers over her head. But that wouldn't help. It was better to get this over with as soon as possible.

It was no surprise to see Ushig standing on the pavement. His dark hair reached to his shoulders, framing deep-set eyes and a narrow nose. The face he wore was slightly longer than a normal human face. He was taller too, thought Ellen, although his smooth skin still gave him the look of a boy no older than her brother.

She had to make a real effort to concentrate. Her mind was still worrying away, trying to work out what Ushig was up to. She knew how the kelpie ought to behave — it would persuade its victim to climb on its back and then leap into the water. So why was Ushig so determined to follow them all the way to London, a busy human city, instead of lurking in an isolated spot far from prying eyes? He should have stayed beside that little loch and waited for another victim. Instead, he had followed Davie and seemed unwilling — or unable — to let him go.

Ushig smiled. "Your father and brother invited me to come again." He tilted his head. "Into your home," he added meaningfully.

"*I* didn't invite you," said Ellen. "I don't want you here."

With shaking hands, she pulled the sprig of rowan from her pocket and jammed it as firmly as she could into a crack in the wall. Then she forced herself to meet Ushig's angry eyes as she spoke the charm.

"When the black horse comes kicking among the rocks, rowan and red thread will close the locks."

Her heart thudding — invisibly, she hoped — she placed both hands on the iron gate and swung it shut. Then she turned and walked back inside on trembling legs.

"Be very careful, little sister," said a soft voice behind her. "The rowan is not a toy. And this is not a game."

Chapter 6

Ellen knew there was only one person she could talk to. Just before the train left Edinburgh, it had been obvious that Aunt Marian knew — or at least suspected — something. But getting hold of her wasn't easy. She didn't have an answering machine. Or a mobile. Or a computer. She only answered the phone when she felt like it. Ellen bit her lip, thinking hard. A letter wasn't the fastest way in the world, but it was all she could think of.

She spent the morning surrounded by balled-up scraps of paper. She was supposed to be writing a book review, an impossible task since she hadn't actually read the book. Writing to Aunt Marian was almost as hard. Somehow she couldn't transfer the words in her head on to the paper in front of her.

She chewed on her pen, thinking about how Ushig had managed to follow them home. Somebody must have told him where they lived and how to get there. It wasn't her and it wasn't Aunt Marian. That left only one other person.

Ellen threw down her pen and headed for the door. She found Davie lying on his bed, his arms crossed behind his head. He flicked a brief glance in her direction then went back to staring at the ceiling.

"Davie," she said, "I need to talk to you."

He looked at her for a moment, then leaned over and pressed a button. Music filled the room. He kept his finger on the button until the sound was bouncing off the walls. He couldn't hear her now, no matter how hard she shouted.

Defeated, she retreated to her own room, where she chewed her pen and stared down at yet another blank sheet of paper. What she really wanted was to pour out all her fears and misgivings, starting right from the moment beside the loch when she had realized what Ushig really was, but whenever she tried to write, the words wouldn't come.

In the end, she simply wrote a brief note, telling her aunt that the boy from Aldhammer had appeared outside their house. Surely even that simple fact would be odd enough to interest Marian. The rest she could leave till later.

Ellen sighed as she slid the letter inside an envelope and sealed it shut. She wished she could persuade herself that Ushig was gone, leaving her and Davie in peace. But the faint hope that her wish might come true vanished when she left the house to post the letter and saw Davie a little way ahead of her, his hood pulled low over his head as though he didn't want to be noticed. He must have left the house just before she did.

He turned on to the High Street and she quickened her pace, rounding the corner just in time to see him slip down the alley beside the supermarket. Cautiously, Ellen followed. She peeked round the corner. Davie was standing in the middle of a deserted delivery yard staring intently at the back wall of the building. Whatever he was looking at, he was concentrating too hard to notice her.

Ellen twisted her head to see what held his attention and gasped in surprise. A blot of darkness was moving up the wall. It reached the top and slid over the parapet like a thick stream of treacle. Moments later, a boy she recognized appeared on the roof. Davie grinned and moved forward. Ushig held out an arm. Ellen watched it twist out of shape, growing longer and thinner, forming a black rope that eventually snaked all the way down to the ground.

"No, Davie," she whispered, as she saw her brother take hold of the rope with both hands and begin to walk his way up the wall. Heart thudding, afraid to call out in case he lost concentration and fell, she watched him work his way higher and higher until he reached the roof and scrambled over the parapet. Then both boys disappeared. She waited for a long time, but they didn't come back.

It wasn't until much later in the afternoon that the rhythmic thump of a football hitting the garden wall told her that Davie was home again. She moved across her bedroom to the window, noting with relief that he was on his own.

"Ellie!" said an irritated voice behind her. "You're not listening!"

"Sorry." She turned back to Rose, who was sitting on Ellen's bed, surrounded by holiday photographs. "I'm just worried about Davie."

"Why?" Rose began gathering up the photos. "He seems fine to me."

Ellen shrugged. There wasn't much she could say. "He's just ... out all the time — and he won't tell me where he's been."

Rose looked up, interested. "Maybe he's got a girlfriend!"

The thumping noise from outside stopped. A few moments later, they heard the front door slam.

"Let's follow him!" Rose jumped to her feet.

Ellen thought about it. It wasn't a bad idea. If she was with Rose and something strange happened, there would be at least one other person who knew what was going on.

Her hopes were dashed as soon as they rounded the corner and found Davie waiting for them at the underpass leading to the huge expanse of lumpy grass that everyone called the marsh.

"What are you two up to?" he asked crossly. "Are you following me?"

Rose giggled and Davie frowned.

"What's so funny?"

"Nothing's funny," said Ellen. "I just wanted to make sure Ushig wasn't around."

Davie snorted. "How could he possibly be here?"

"I've seen him, Davie." Ellen stared hard at her brother. "He's here. I saw him on the street — and I've seen him with you."

"I don't know who you saw," said Davie dismissively, "but it wasn't that boy from Aldhammer. How could it be?"

"You're right." Rose spoke quietly, trying to keep things calm. "We *were* following you — but it was just a bit of fun, wasn't it Ellie?"

Red-faced with annoyance, Ellen glared at her

brother. "No," she said. "It's not just a bit of fun."

Rose forced a smile and laid a hand on Ellen's arm. "Let's go," she said.

"Oh, what's the point?" Ellen turned away in disgust.

Ellen nodded in all the right places as she and Rose made their way to school next morning, but she wasn't really paying attention. She was watching Davie hurry along in front of them, oddly eager for the school gates to close around him for another year.

She waved goodbye as he turned into the senior school, cheered by the thought that Ushig couldn't get near him while he was in school. Maybe the water wraith would lose interest in her brother now he had a whole city to explore.

All the way home, Rose talked non-stop about their new project. Mrs Grandison wanted everyone to have a go at tracing their ancestors. Rose was full of enthusiasm. Almost all her family lived nearby. It wouldn't be so easy for Ellen, though. Dad's parents lived in Ireland and didn't visit very often. As for Mum and Aunt Marian, Ellen was surprised to realize she didn't even know their mother's first name. She couldn't ever remember them talking much about her.

When they reached the senior school playground, Ellen saw Davie crouched among a group of boys huddled together near the back wall. His shirt tail was flapping loose and his new jacket lay discarded on the ground.

Whatever the boys were up to, it was absorbing all their attention. Ellen saw a teacher appear on the steps and move towards them. When the teacher arrived, there were only two boys left. One of them was Davie. Ellen stared hard at the other one and felt a sudden sinking sensation in the pit of her stomach.

The boy looked perfectly ordinary, dressed in a white shirt, grey trousers and black blazer, no different from any of the others — except for the streaks of green in his long dark hair.

Chapter 7

Ellen took a couple of steps forward.

At that moment, Davie spotted them hovering beside the gate. An angry frown darkened his face. He turned and said something to Ushig, then he began to walk towards them. Ushig looked across at Ellen and she saw his face grow still and watchful, like the surface of a pool on a calm day. She shivered at the thought.

As Davie moved across the playground Ushig turned and walked off in the opposite direction. The teacher stared after him for a long moment before he turned and headed back inside the building.

"What are you two doing here? You're supposed to go straight home from school."

"I'm waiting for you, Davie." Ellen ignored Rose, who was nervously plucking at her sleeve.

A couple of boys walked past. One of them sniggered. "What's this Davie?" he said. "Your escort?"

Davie's face darkened. "Get lost, Neil."

"You told me he wasn't here!" Ellen snapped.

"Who?" Davie turned to look at Ushig, who was disappearing round the corner of the building. "That's just one of the new boys in my year."

Ellen felt her face grow hot. "Don't lie to me, Davie!"

"Let's go, Ellen." Rose spoke in an embarrassed whisper. "Don't make a fuss."

She tugged at Ellen's arm. Ellen resisted, determined that Davie was going to tell her what was really going on, but it was obvious from the equally determined look on her brother's face that making a scene would get her nowhere. Her insides churning with a mixture of fear and anger, she allowed Rose to lead her away.

Rose began talking softly and insistently, as though it was Ellen who was behaving oddly. "But it's *not* me," she said to herself. "Davie's in trouble and I have to help him, whether he wants me to or not." Her brother had no protection against a water wraith like Ushig. Without Robert Kirk's book, neither would Ellen. She would not have known what Ushig was, or what he had been about to do. Davie could so easily have ended up floating among the weeds beneath the surface of that woodland pool. Her stomach heaved again at the thought.

She hiked her bag higher on her shoulder and set off for home, too distracted by the thoughts rushing around inside her head to listen to Rose. She still hadn't managed to work out how Ushig had followed them here, but she was sure now that Davie had helped him — was still helping him. Where was Ushig hiding when he wasn't with Davie? Although, if he could change his shape whenever he pleased, he could probably go just about anywhere as long as he wore someone else's face and body.

Ellen barely noticed when she said goodbye to Rose. She was thinking about her book. It had saved Davie once before. It was the only thing that could help her now. She dropped her bag in the hall and hurried upstairs, barely taking the time to call out a hello to her mother.

There was a notice on Davie's bedroom door. It hadn't been there yesterday. "KEEP OUT!" it said, in big black letters. "THIS MEANS YOU!"

"Not this time," Ellen said to herself. She pushed her glasses up her nose and opened the door. Davie was at his desk, pen in hand, surrounded by books and paper. But Ellen wasn't fooled. None of the books were open.

"Where's he been hiding, Davie? And why did you do it? Why did you bring him here? I know it was you."

Davie slid a sheet of paper out of sight, but not before she saw what he had been drawing — a horse with a human head. Ushig's head.

"I don't know what you're talking about. And I've got things to do."

Ellen stood her ground. "It's no use, Davie," she said. "I've seen him three times now. You told me I imagined it all!"

Her cheeks grew hot with anger when she thought of how Davie had made her look like a fool. "You told me it was all rubbish!"

Davie flicked his pen from side to side and then he grinned. "Well," he said. "You've got to admit it was easier just to let you think we'd left him behind."

Ellen made a huge effort. It wouldn't help at all if she lost her temper. "That thing drowns people," she said, determined not to be sidetracked. She tried to speak slowly and reasonably. "It wants you, Davie. It's just waiting for its chance."

"You're right, Ellen." Davie swung round to face her. "He does want me, but not the way you mean. He's just interested in what it's like to be human. He asked me to help him and I said yes."

Flick, flick, flick, went the pen. Ellen stepped forward and snatched it out of his hand. "This is serious, Davie," she said. "You know that creature is dangerous."

Davie frowned and grabbed it back. "Don't be such a baby," he snapped. "Ushig's not scary once you get used to him." He smiled up at her. "Remember the fat man we had to squeeze past on the way to the buffet? That was him! The guard never noticed there were two of them!"

"But how did he know where we were going?" Ellen remembered their last day in Aldhammer. Ushig hadn't known that they were leaving the next morning and once they were indoors there had been no opportunity afterwards for Davie to tell him. She had made sure of that.

Davie shrugged. "Ushig and me, we're sort of linked. He says he can feel where I am. It's like a ... thread that joins us together."

"Linked?" Ellen looked at him, horrified. "Davie, can't you remember anything about what happened at the loch? Don't you remember how scared we were? And now you're saying he can find you any time he likes!"

"Okay," said Davie. "Maybe I can't remember much about what happened then. I don't know why. But he's been showing me all kinds of things — amazing stuff! He's really interesting, Ellen. In the playground, he was turning his hand into all sorts of different shapes. The others thought it was just a trick, but it wasn't — it was real! One of the boys in my class skipped off lessons for the afternoon and Ushig took his place!"

Ellen frowned. Whatever her brother thought, this was not a game. Ushig had told her so himself. She tried again. "Davie, please —"

He wasn't listening. "They all think it's hypnosis or something." His eyes glittered. "And all he wants in exchange is for someone to explain things to him. He's never seen a city before!"

"Davie," begged Ellen, "please stay away from him. If you don't, I'm going to tell Mum and Dad."

Davie laughed. "Tell them what? That there's a bogeyman after us? You really do have some imagination." He sat back in his chair and looked up at her. "Remember the dragon with the big orange eyes that kept looking in through your bedroom window? Mum had to take you outside in the dark to show you it was just the streetlight!"

"That's not fair Davie! I was only six!"

"All the same, it's not you she's likely to believe, is it? Not with a story like that."

Ellen bit her lip. The scorn in her brother's voice scared her. It was like talking to a stranger. Davie was sometimes annoying, but he was never this mean.

He turned back to his desk, pulled out the piece of paper and added a wild scribble of mane to the human head.

She stared at him, worried by the manic gleam in his eye. Maybe Ushig really was interested in the human world, but there was something about the way he looked at the people around him that made her feel uncomfortable. It was the same look she had seen on the faces of people watching animals at the zoo.

"I keep telling you, Ellen," said Davie. "He really doesn't mean any harm. If you don't believe me, why don't you talk to him yourself?"

"Because I don't know where he is." She didn't want to admit that her heart thumped and her legs turned to rubber every time Ushig was near.

"He's at the tow path beside the canal. In the woods."

"But you're not allowed over there any more."

At the start of the summer holiday, Davie and some friends had built a ramshackle hut out of old boards in the trees beside the canal, but their fun came to an abrupt halt when one of them hitched a sneaky ride on a barge and was hauled home in disgrace by the police. Law-abiding Davie hadn't been there at the time, but that didn't stop Mum and Dad from having a very serious talk with him, ending with an absolute ban on going near the canal again without an adult.

"Guilt by association," Davie had told Ellen resentfully. "Someone else does something wrong and I get into trouble."

Davie glared. "So? Ushig needed someplace to stay. I couldn't exactly give him a tent in the garden, could I?" He tossed his pen on to the table and reached underneath for his bag. "I'm going over there later ... just as soon as I finish my homework." He looked up at his sister. She saw him frown as though he was trying to work something out. "Ushig doesn't mean any harm but things can get a bit wild when he's around ... maybe it's better if you stay away."

"What do you mean, 'wild'?" demanded Ellen, though by now she had a pretty good idea.

"Oh ... just stuff. Nothing too dangerous, if that's what you're getting at." A brief smile flickered across Davie's face and his eyes took on that strange, faraway look that worried her so much.

She tried to drag his attention back to her. "Why can't you tell me then, if it's not dangerous?"

But Davie just bent his head over his books without bothering to answer.

"You're so taken with him you can't even think straight."

Davie continued to ignore her and after a moment, Ellen left him to it. It was obvious that nothing she could say would make any difference. She sighed heavily as she made her way downstairs. Marian was unreachable and Davie had made it very clear that it was no good talking to Mum or Dad. This was something she had to deal with on her own.

Chapter 8

If she slowed down, even for a second, Ellen knew her courage would falter and she wouldn't be able to carry on through the underpass and across the marsh to the canal. She hunched into her jacket and kept her head low as she crossed the grass. She wasn't allowed over here on her own either. If she met anyone who knew her, she would be turned around and marched back to face Mum and Dad.

She stepped through a gap in the railings and on to the narrow bridge over the canal lock. Beneath her, a boat was slowly rising inside the lock gates. Water rushed into the narrow space between the boat and the walls. Plastic cups, beer cans and other rubbish surfaced for a brief moment before they disappeared beneath the grey frothy bubbles.

She couldn't understand how her brother could bear to be this close to the canal in the company of that creature. But then, he wasn't the Davie she was used to. Not any more. Davie was the reliable one, the one who could be trusted not to daydream himself lost, or lose track of time. His secretive behaviour, his wild enthusiasm for Ushig — and his absolute determination not to listen when

Ellen tried to talk to him about the wraith — was nothing like her cautious, dependable brother.

He certainly wasn't dependable any more. Ellen bit her lip. She was sure it wasn't Davie's fault. Ushig had done something to him. Nobody knew anything about it ... except her. Whether Davie appreciated it or not, she wasn't going to give up without a fight.

She slipped her hand into her pocket, taking comfort from the crumbling rowan twigs, as she forced one foot in front of the other, all the way along the towpath until she arrived at a stand of spindly trees. This was where the boys had made their camp. Taking a deep breath, she ducked under the branches and slipped and slithered her way down a slope littered with last year's leaves.

She found Ushig in the open space at the bottom, sitting cross-legged in front of a rough shelter made from bits of wood and plastic bin liners. In front of him were the blackened remains of a camp fire.

He watched her look around, noting the scatter of belongings, the sleeping bag, the books and other bits and pieces. Davie's precious camera was there, lying in the dirt.

Ellen had heard people say they were so frightened that their knees knocked together, but it had never happened to her. Not until now. It took a huge effort to persuade her wobbly legs to carry her forward. "All this stuff belongs to my brother," she said. "Why did he give it to you?"

Ushig rose to his feet and took a step towards her. Ellen had to tilt her head to look up at him.

He was definitely taller than before. She forced herself not to step back.

"They are gifts," he said. "Is it not right to accept gifts?"

"They're not gifts if you make people hand them over," said Ellen, her voice quavering.

Ushig's lips thinned. "I did not ask for these things."

Ellen took a deep breath. None of the stuff Davie had brought here was important. It was Davie who mattered. "You tried to drown him."

"But I did not," said Ushig.

"Because you couldn't!" Ellen was sure Davie had escaped only because of the charm she still carried, hidden beneath her school shirt. "You said you meant no harm but you did — you still do!"

Ushig's brow furrowed in concentration, like someone trying to follow a language they didn't fully understand. "It is not in my nature to lie," he said at last. "I told you I mean you no harm and that is true. There is no lie there that I can see."

And suddenly Ellen understood. She should have realized it before. Her book warned over and over again that the Peerie Folk were tricky. He had said he meant *her* no harm. Not Davie. Only her.

"I only act as I was made to act." Ushig looked at Ellen with an avid curiosity that made her shiver. "Your kind interests me. There was one I met before. He came into my world as I came into yours."

Ellen's eyes opened wide in surprise. So it was true. Robert Kirk's book was not a story. It was real.

He settled himself back on the ground. "Your brother told me of the book that was made. He also told me it gives you great delight." He was stirring the blackened embers of the fire with a twig. Ellen watched his hand go round and round, round and round.

"Surely you would like to know more?"

She opened her mouth to deny it, then closed it again. Not so long ago, it would have been a dream come true. A chance to meet the Brown Man of the Moors, guardian of the wild places, or Loreag the Spinner, who would make you a magic cloak in exchange for the gift of milk.

Absently, she took hold of the charm and twisted it between her fingers, thinking of the girl on the shore and that sense of delight and wonder when she first realized she was talking to a real live selkie. Then she thought of the other, darker things in the world he came from.

She shook her head, trying to clear her thoughts. "How did he get there?" she asked. "The man who wrote the book?"

"The Queen had a fancy for a human child to serve her," said Ushig. "She made a fetch, a creature of twigs and grass, charged with power enough to imitate life — for a while, at least. That was what was left in this world when the child was taken. The Queen made much of him, dressed him in cloth of gold, had him sit on a cushion at her feet ... until she grew weary of him." He tossed the twig away and looked up at her.

"What queen?" There was no mention of any queen in Ellen's book.

"He did not write of the Queen of the Night?" Ushig looked at her in surprise for a moment, then he shrugged. "Perhaps he had good reason to forget her."

"He must have managed to escape though," said Ellen. "He was back in this world when he wrote his book."

Ushig let loose what sounded like a genuine laugh. "No one escapes the Queen's court. The child grew tiresome and she left him to rot." His eyes narrowed. "But you are right. Somehow he managed to find his way home again."

"The book ends when he reached the sea," said Ellen. "It doesn't tell how he found his way back." And even if it did, she thought to herself, I wouldn't tell *you*.

"Everyone has their secrets," said Ushig. His head tilted to one side, he gave her a measuring look. "Perhaps you might like to share some of mine?"

The harsh call of a magpie interrupted him. He slid his gaze towards the branches above him, where two birds sat side by side, both staring down. He looked back at Ellen, his eyes sparkling with excitement.

"Would you like to know their speech?"

The birds shifted restlessly from foot to foot. "Not man," said the one on the left.

"Not horse," said the other. It took to the air and flapped heavily away, quickly followed by its companion.

Ellen blinked. Had she really heard those words? She looked at Ushig, surprised to realize he was on his feet, much closer than before. When had that happened?

"There was a promise made," he said softly. "Your brother has shown me his world. And I have agreed to show him my own. It will be a grand adventure."

"No!" Ushig was trying to fill her head with nonsense, just as he had done with her brother. This creature was old and clever, tempting her with possibilities, telling her things she wanted to hear. She pulled out the charm.

Ushig's lips twisted in amusement. "There was a promise made," he repeated.

"I made that promise to save my brother's life," snapped Ellen. "It doesn't count."

He frowned. "Why do you care for him so much?"

"Davie's always looked out for me and now I'm looking out for him. He needs my help."

Ushig stared at her. "Is this loyalty? Or love? I would like to learn about love."

Ellen seized her chance. Maybe if she could make Ushig understand what Davie meant to her, then he would let him go.

"Davie's my family," she said slowly, searching for the right words. "Mum and Dad, Davie and me, we're family. So is Aunt Marian." She searched the alien face for signs of understanding. "We belong together. We look after each other — and we love each other."

Ushig nodded. "I came here and fought my nature to understand these things."

Ellen wasn't convinced. Ushig hadn't stopped himself from taking Davie at the loch. It was the charm round her neck that had saved her brother. She looked down, surprised to see it lying in the palm of her hand. When had she taken it off? Quickly, she slipped it back over her head.

"This world is different from mine." Ushig's face grew thoughtful. "We have no dawn, no dusk. There is no light except that bestowed by the Lady. Days do not pass there as they do here. Our bodies are made differently from yours. Some among us have been there since time began."

Ellen knew it was vital not to be distracted by that soft, persuasive voice. She clenched her jaw and stared back at him.

He watched her closely for a moment then, to her relief, he backed away and sat down again beside the cold embers of the fire. "Tell me," he asked. "What happened to the one who wrote the book?"

"I don't know," said Ellen. "It was a long time ago. I suppose he died."

"Death," said Ushig slowly. "Do you suppose I might taste death?" He smiled. "And what about you, Ellen? What do you want?"

Keeping a tight hold of the charm, Ellen said, "I want you to go away."

"But I like this world." Ushig grinned. "I could be a king here ... or a rich man. These things are mine for the taking."

"Why don't you take them, then?" Ellen said sourly. "Just leave me and Davie alone."

The grin disappeared and once more she sensed the alien creature looking out from inside the boy's body.

"Not yet," he said. "I cannot have what I want. There is a price I have not paid."

"What price?"

But he only shook his head.

"Please," she begged. "Please, Ushig. Leave my brother alone."

Ushig's eyes flickered red and Ellen suddenly found her own eyes locked on his. The face in front of her blurred, the nose and forehead melting together to form a solid shelf of bone. His body fell towards her and she tilted her head, looking up at the dark shape that filled her vision. The huge black horse snorted and stamped the ground and she felt the earth shake beneath those massive hooves. The darkness grew, spreading itself across her vision until the world disappeared and there was nothing but darkness — and those fiery pinpoints of crimson light.

"What is your price, little sister?" The voice howled around her like a nightmare wind. "What will you pay for your brother's life?"

The last shreds of her courage dissolved away to nothing. Ellen turned and fled.

Chapter 9

Ellen stared at the explosion of colour across her bed. She hadn't worn the ribbons for a long time but Mum had tucked them away in a corner of a drawer in case they were ever needed — and Ellen did need them, though not for any purpose her mother might have imagined.

The book lay open on the bed. Ellen reached out and ran her finger across the words beneath the picture of the boy and the kelpie.

"This thing lived by trickery and fed on fear. But my friendly shadow had set me free from the illusions woven by such creatures. I watched the gleam of anticipation in its eyes turn to wary suspicion when it realized what it was I held in my hand."

Ellen peered down at the picture. She had always thought the boy was holding a length of rope, but it wasn't. She was sure now that the thing swinging from his hand was a homemade bridle.

She turned her attention back to the silky ribbons and lifted up a soft handful of reds, greens, blues and golds. The selkie had told her to think of Ushig as she wove. Well, that wasn't difficult. She couldn't stop thinking about him.

There was a tap at the door. She looked up to see Davie step inside. "Ellen," he said carefully. "I really don't think you should come with me to see Ushig."

She reached for a scarlet ribbon. "Don't worry about it. I've still got my own homework to do. And it's nearly dinner time."

Davie glanced at his watch. "So it is."

His voice was casual, but Ellen could hear the undertone of relief. She wondered what it must feel like to be Davie, his brain split in two between the wild excitement generated by the water wraith and his strong sense of responsibility towards Ellen. He had convinced himself that Ushig wasn't dangerous and yet, at the same time, he didn't want him anywhere near his sister.

He lifted one of the ribbons and began to smooth it between his fingers. "What are you doing?"

"Nothing." She pulled a loose thread from the ribbon in her hand. Ushig would not be able to fool Davie forever and when he finally found out the truth, Ellen would have a weapon ready to put in his hand. "Why didn't you tell me Ushig was here?"

Davie shrugged. "Because I knew you'd be like this." He dropped the ribbon and sat on the end of her bed, tapping his fingers restlessly against the bedpost. "I always thought it was silly, when you went on about magic," he said, "but Ushig is different."

He jumped up and began to pace the floor. Ellen watched him, uneasy at the sight of his manic energy.

"He's like an alien, from another planet, and we're the ones who found him." Davie's face was flushed, as though his body burned with fever.

"Davie," she said. "Do you remember our last day in Aldhammer? Did Aunt Marian tell you we saw a seal?" Ellen knew she had to keep trying, even though it was becoming very clear that Davie would not listen.

He blinked in surprise. "Yeah."

"It wasn't a seal," she said. "It was a selkie. A seal woman. She warned me to have nothing to do with Ushig. She said, whatever he wants, it's nothing good."

Davie smiled. "Look, Ellen, I was wrong, okay? Some of the things in that book of yours are real. But now you're telling me they're popping up all over the place." He shook his head. "I don't think so."

Ellen glared at him. "How can you be so stupid? That thing works out what you want and then he tempts you with it. He's dangerous, Davie!"

She threw down the ribbons and reached for her book. "So are these. This one," she flicked the pages over and pointed at a hooded shape hunched over the oars of a rowing boat. "This is the Finman. If you get in that boat, you'll be lucky if you ever get out again. "Listen!"

She began to read aloud. *"The dark shape turned towards me and crooked a finger, beckoning me forward. But I had heard others speak of this creature. I would not choose to step into that boat with that ferryman. The cloaked and hooded figure that waited so patiently on the water was not human — and his boat was not a boat. It was a mouth."*

Ellen looked up. Davie glanced at the book and then away, his eyes travelling aimlessly round the room. She clenched her teeth and persevered, holding out another picture of a man shape standing on a hill, wearing a huge crown of antlers. A pack of skinny, red-eyed dogs crouched at his feet. "That's the Wild Hunt, Davie."

"Well," Davie said dismissively, making for the door. "You don't have to worry, do you? It's not your company Ushig wants. It's mine."

Ellen clenched her fists. "I won't let you do this, Davie."

He spun round, his face twisted into a scowl. "I'm warning you, Ellen, don't get in my way. You'll be sorry if you try."

She stared at him, shocked by the intensity of his anger. He glared at her for a long moment.

"Why are you doing this Davie? Why are you so obsessed with Ushig?"

Davie glared. "You're the one that's obsessed, Ellen. You've got things all upside down but you just can't see it."

A dreadful suspicion crept into Ellen's head. Maybe it was already too late. This wasn't the brother she knew. Maybe it wasn't Davie at all, but some other creature. A changeling, or a shapeshifter, like Ushig. Her heart lurched.

"Davie," she said in a small, soft voice.

He stopped in the doorway. "What?"

"Do you remember when I was small and Mum used to sing me to sleep?" Ellen was on edge, holding her breath.

"Of course I do!" Davie looked at her, puzzled.

"I used to open your bedroom door and beg her to stop!"

Ellen smiled weakly. "She does have the most awful voice, doesn't she?"

As Davie left the room, Ellen placed the book carefully on her shelf, picked up a handful of ribbons and tied a knot in one end. Ushig had to be stopped. That strange glitter in her brother's eyes was like an infection raging out of control.

She looked down at the colours in her hand. Such a fragile weapon, but it was better than nothing at all. Putting everything out of her mind except the creature they were meant to snare, she began to braid a shiny, multi-coloured rope.

"You two seem to have swapped personalities," Mum said when they were downstairs, waiting for dinner. She looked from one side of the table to the other. Armed with a pile of felt tips, Davie was drawing a line of odd-looking horses emerging from a saucer-shaped spaceship while Ellen sat opposite him, carefully organising a collection of family photographs into different piles.

Davie threw his pen on the table and jumped to his feet, sending his chair toppling. "There's nothing wrong with me! I'd be fine if she just stopped following me around all the time!"

Mum frowned as she watched Davie snatch up his pens and paper and head out the door. She turned to Ellen. "Is he right? Are you following him?"

"No!" Ellen snapped, still smarting from the way Davie had behaved upstairs.

Her mother pulled out a chair and sat down beside her. "I know you've always been good friends," she said gently, "but Davie's getting older now. He needs time on his own."

"But ..." Ellen's voice rose in protest.

Her mother smiled. "Don't worry Ellen, you'll have the old Davie back again. Just give him a bit more space for the moment, all right?"

Knowing that it was hopeless, Ellen opened her mouth to try again, but shut it when the phone began to ring.

Mum reached out to answer it. "Marian!" Her voice lifted in pleasure and surprise.

Ellen felt a sudden surge of hope. Surely there could be only one reason for Aunt Marian to call?

A puzzled frown appeared on her mother's face. "The Crafts Council? In London? But you never ..." She listened some more, then said, "No, no, that's great." She held the phone out to Ellen. "Marian wants to talk to you."

Eagerly, Ellen reached for the phone.

"Is Laura still in the room?" The voice that echoed in her ear was hard and urgent. It didn't sound like Marian at all.

"Yes." Ellen glanced at her mother, who was unashamedly listening in.

"Then don't talk, Ellen. Just listen."

"But ..."

"I'll be with you tomorrow afternoon. I want you to promise me you won't go anywhere near that creature before I get there."

"Aunt Marian, it's not me —"

"Promise me, Ellen!"

Ellen sighed. This conversation was not going the way she had hoped. Aware of her mother's eyes on her face, she forced herself to smile. "I promise, Aunt Marian."

"I'll see you tomorrow, then," said Marian. "And remember. Stay away from him. You and Davie both."

There was a click and the line went dead. Ellen handed the phone back to her mother.

"So, what's the promise then?"

"Nothing much," Ellen thought quickly. "A secret. A surprise." Both of those things were true, at least.

"Well I suppose I'll find out eventually." Laura smiled at her daughter. "It's enough of a surprise to get a visit from my sister!"

Weak with relief, Ellen smiled back. Only one more day and Aunt Marian would be here. She would know what to do. Everything was going to be all right.

Mum reached out for one of the photographs on the table. "How's it going?"

"Not bad," said Ellen. "I've got lots of stuff from Dad's side, but I'm stuck on yours. I don't even know your mother's first name, or what she was called before she got married."

Mum dropped the photo. "There's nothing much to tell. Your grandmother drowned. I was thirteen and Marian was ten. I don't remember much about it."

Ellen looked disbelievingly at her mother. "You can't even remember her name? I'd remember everything about you."

Her mother placed the photograph carefully on the table and stood up. "Of course I remember! Her name was Aisil." She walked stiffly across the room, turned on the oven and then walked all the way back to open a drawer.

"That's an odd name," said Ellen, hoping for more, disappointed when her mother said nothing. She put her elbow on the table and cupped her chin in her hand. "What else do you remember?"

Laura paused with one hand still in the drawer. "Well ... she wasn't much good at the basic stuff. Our house was always a mess. She was a lot more like Marian than me." A small smile tugged the corners of her mouth. "She was kind, though. And gentle. With us, anyway." The smile disappeared. "Not so much with Dad."

Ellen watched her mother close the drawer without taking anything out. She looked around, as though she had lost track of what she was doing.

"Is that why you never go to Aldhammer?" asked Ellen. "Because your mother died? Aunt Marian said you had reasons, but she said we had to ask you."

Her mother stiffened and Ellen realized she was pushing her luck, but she didn't want to stop. "Never wanting to go home isn't really — "she paused. It didn't seem a good idea to say it wasn't normal."

"I just don't like the sea," said Mum. She opened the drawer again, pulled out a handful of cutlery and dumped it on the table in a heap.

Ellen hurried to gather up her photographs. "But Aldhammer is where you grew up." She couldn't imagine not wanting to come back here and visit her friends if she ever moved away.

"Oh, Ellen." Her mother's voice trembled. "It wasn't like that." She hesitated, then sat down at the table again. "Dad did his best, but Mum was always a bit odd. He used to bring her flowers, or little presents, but she never seemed happy."

Ellen couldn't remember much about her grandfather other than a warm, comforting presence, but she was sure Mum was right. He had been kind.

Her mother's voice hardened. "She didn't seem to care, though. The only time I ever saw her smile at him was when he gave her that book you've got upstairs."

"What did she look like?"

With a visible effort, Laura focused on her daughter. "Her eyes were brown, like yours."

"And yours, too."

Mum nodded. "She used to spend a lot of time on the shore. She would sit there for hours, even in the rain. Dad used to send me or Marian to fetch her back. And then, one day, she wasn't there."

"Was there an accident? Did she drown?" Ellen could see the effort it was costing her mother to talk about it, but she wanted to know.

She watched her mother fiddle with the knives and forks. When she looked up at Ellen, her eyes were bright with unshed tears. "Mum would never go in the water. I don't think she could swim. They found her clothes, all neatly folded on top of the rocks. It wasn't an accident, Ellen."

"Oh, Mum!" Ellen reached for her mother's hand.

"That's why Marian spends so much time on the shore." Her mother gave a watery smile. "When she was younger, she used to say Mum talked to her there. But I haven't been near the shore. Not once, since the day Mum died."

She turned away. "So now you know why I don't go to Aldhammer and why I don't like the sea. Now give Davie a shout. It's time for dinner."

Ellen climbed the stairs and pushed open the door to Davie's bedroom. His jacket was slung over the back of his chair and the drawing pad was on his desk. A scatter of felt tips lay across it, but there was no sign of her brother.

Frowning, Ellen reached out and plucked a coarse black hair from the sleeve of his jacket. Moving much faster now, she hurried downstairs and checked the other rooms. Davie wasn't there. He wasn't anywhere in the house.

Chapter 10

Mum lifted the phone and dialled Davie's number. Ellen heard the faint sound of tinny music from upstairs as she slammed the phone back down.

"Go and fetch him, Ellen," she snapped. "He can't be far away — and tell him his little sister's going to be following him around a lot more closely if he can't be trusted to turn up on time for meals."

Ellen hurried out of the house, almost falling over Rose, who was outside on the pavement, hanging on to her dog, Spanner. He strained forward, wagging his tail in delight when he saw Ellen.

"I was just going to knock for you." Rose gave a tentative smile as the dog danced round her, tangling its lead in her legs. "I thought we could take Spanner for a walk together."

"I'm going to get Davie." Ellen walked on without stopping. "Mum asked me to fetch him. He's over at the canal."

Rose unwound herself from the lead and hurried to catch up with Ellen. "I thought he wasn't allowed over there."

"He's not." She knew there was no point in trying to explain. She didn't have time and Rose wouldn't believe her anyway.

Rose allowed Spanner to drag her forward. "I'll come with you, if you like."

She fell into step beside Ellen as she rushed along the road and through the underpass. Spanner eagerly took the lead, but halfway along the track to the canal, he began to slow down. Rose looked at him in surprise as he began to growl. Not long afterwards, he sat down and refused to move on. Rose hauled on the lead, almost choking the dog in her efforts to keep him moving, but it was no use. Spanner wasn't going anywhere — and Ellen thought she knew why. It wasn't the water he was afraid of. It was Ushig.

"Let's go back," Rose coaxed. "Spanner wants to go and Davie's sensible. He'll be home soon."

Ellen shook her head and shaded her eyes with her hand, searching the wide empty expanse of the marsh, but she saw no sign of Davie. "I don't have any choice, Rose. Mum said not to come back without him." She bit hard on her lip, trying to keep down the rising tide of panic. She couldn't explain. Rose would think she had gone mad.

Rose frowned at her, still struggling to haul Spanner to his feet, then she said, "You can't go over there on your own, Ellie." Her voice was soft and reasonable but there was a wary look in her eye. "Let's tell your mum. She'll know what to do."

Rose reached into her pocket with her free hand and pulled out her phone. Ellen turned away. Then she stopped. Rose was right. She should have thought of this before, not now, when there was almost no time left. If Mum knew Davie was at the canal, he would be banned from the marsh altogether. Tomorrow, Aunt Marian would be here. She would know what to do. It would give Ellen a little more time.

"Good idea! Phone Mum, Rose. Tell her where we've gone — and tell her to come quickly!"

Taking a deep breath, Ellen began to run. She didn't know how long it had been since Davie left the house or how long he had been alone with Ushig, but she was sure that time was running out.

She reached the canal and crossed quickly on to the deserted towpath, shivering as the first stirrings of an evening breeze chilled her skin. She pulled up the zipper of her jacket. By now, Mum would be on her way. A crimson sun was setting slowly in the west, sending streaks of red across the sky. Very soon now, it would be dark.

A burst of wild laughter broke the silence and she felt her heart jump in her chest. It was answered by a noise that could only have come from Ushig. She reached the trees and stopped to peer through the branches.

Her brother was there, but there was no sign of the pale-faced boy with the sardonic smile. Instead, Davie was looking up at the massive shape of a coal black horse. Ellen watched him reach out and bury his hands in the flowing mane. Then, with one smooth movement, he was on its back.

"No Davie!" Ellen half ran, half fell down the slope, ignoring the branches that whipped across her face. It was too late now to look for help from Mum or Aunt Marian, too late for anyone else. She was on her own.

She burst into the clearing and the horse stepped sideways, momentarily startled by her abrupt arrival. When it turned to face her, she saw triumph burning in its eyes.

The earth shook as its hooves stamped the ground, but Ellen was focused only on her brother. A bolt of fear shot through her body at the look of eager anticipation on his face.

Pulling the makeshift bridle from her pocket, she threw it as hard as she could. It flew across the space between them as the horse reared up into the air with Davie on its back.

Hooves thudded into the ground. The horse stopped moving. Ellen watched the fire in its eyes slowly die, the flimsy, multi-coloured rope dangling from one coal black ear. She felt no sense of relief. One twitch of the horse's head and it would fall off. It was a fragile protection against such a powerful beast.

Fragile or not, it had worked. She felt a sudden rush of gratitude towards the selkie girl who had risked leaving the safety of the sea to help her. But she still had to persuade Davie to get off the creature's back.

Her brother was glaring at her, his face red with anger. "What are you doing here?" He looked from her to the bridle and back again. "What have you done?"

Fighting her fear, Ellen moved forward to where the horse stood silent and obedient. It snorted and she jumped back in alarm, but it simply looked at her with mild bemusement.

"Let my brother go," she whispered. Her body

quivered and her voice shook, but she couldn't afford to give in to weakness. "Let him go. Now."

Hardly daring to believe it, she saw the horse lower its head, stretch out one leg and bend gracefully towards the ground.

There had been no time to work out anything beyond the moment when she threw the bridle, but Ellen didn't care. All that mattered was to make sure her brother was off the horse and safely back on the ground.

"Davie," she pleaded, "you can come down now. The bridle will keep you safe. Please come down."

She reached up to fix the braided ribbons more securely round the horse's neck, but her brother clamped his hand over hers before she could touch them.

"You don't understand!" Davie yelled. "He's not going to hurt me! He's taking me to another world! Another world, Ellen!"

"Davie, no!"

But it was too late. He leaned forward and grabbed the bridle that hung so precariously on the horse's head. With one quick gesture, he tossed it on the ground.

Ellen jumped forward and grabbed hold of its mane as she saw fire rekindle in the horse's eyes. With a scream of triumph, it leapt forward, dragging Ellen along with it, tearing through the bushes and across the towpath. There was no time for even a single breath before all three plunged into the murky waters of the canal.

Chapter 11

Ellen blinked up into cool grey light. She was
still alive. She wasn't even wet. Tentatively, she
moved her body and felt the ground change shape
beneath her. It was sand. She was lying on sand.
There was a small hard lump digging into her
left shoulder. She rolled over on to her hands and
knees, reached down and picked up a small brown
pebble. Somehow, its smooth roundness in her
hand made everything else feel a little more real.

It was a relief to look up and see Davie close
by. He was already on his feet, brushing sand off
his clothes. Behind him was Ushig, staring at
Ellen with a puzzled frown on his face. The frown
deepened. She dropped the pebble and looked
away.

"Where are we Davie?"

"It looks like Aldhammer," he said, "but it's not."

He was right. The little bay looked exactly like
the shore at Aldhammer. Ellen's eyes travelled
around the familiar stone outcrops and patches of
gritty sand. Even the curve of the bay looked the
same. There were differences, though. The air felt
heavy, not cool and fresh. No breeze ruffled the
glassy surface of the water. Despite the similarities,
Ellen was sure that she and Davie were a long way
from home.

She turned her head. Instead of the little houses and narrow lanes, the shore was lined with trees. Thin, pale-leaved saplings fought for space beneath ancient giants, some hunched close to the ground with wide spreading branches, others soaring so high that Ellen had to bend her head all the way back to look up at them. This was a forest that no human hand had ever touched. She squinted up at the grey cloudless sky. There was no sign of the sun.

"Oh, Davie," sighed Ellen. "What have you done?"

Her brother walked towards her. He was trembling slightly, as though his body was too heavy for his legs. "Come on, Ellen," he reached out a hand and hauled her upright. "Don't you see? This is the journey Ushig saw when he told my fortune. It's another world! Aren't you the least bit interested?"

His eyes jumped from here to there, eagerly drinking in the empty shore and Ellen couldn't help but feel an answering spark of excitement. She tilted her head as a faint, insistent melody floated towards her on the still air and took a couple of steps forward, straining to listen. The music filled her head with promises of safety, of dreams fulfilled and endless rest.

Something hard jabbed into her foot and she looked down to see her glasses lying in the sand. With dawning horror she realized that the music had driven everything from her mind, filling it with the urge to step into that ancient forest and follow the song to its source.

Clapping her hands over her ears, she yelled, "Davie! Don't listen! It's a trap!"

Davie grinned and cocked his head to one side. After a moment he gestured for her to take her hands away. "It's safe now," he said. "The music's stopped."

Slowly, Ellen did as she was bid.

Davie laughed. "I must be trapped already, right?"

"It's not a joke, Davie!" Ellen was deeply frightened by the fact that Ushig's hold over Davie was clearly far stronger than the insistent call from within the forest.

She picked up her glasses, brushed them clean and raised them to her face, but then she stopped. She could see perfectly well without them — even the individual grains of sand on Davie's jeans. Her glasses didn't seem to matter here. All the same, she folded them up and stuffed them in her pocket. They had been part of her for so long she felt naked without them.

"We must go," Ushig said to Davie. "We must walk the Royal Road."

There was a Royal Road near Aldhammer too, Ellen remembered, the route used long ago by kings and queens travelling between Scotland and England. But that road led through quiet country lanes, not through this ancient woodland.

Ushig's odd-coloured eyes flickered between forest and shore. He seemed wary — almost nervous. Ellen shivered. If the wraith felt threatened here, what did that mean for her and Davie?

She darted a nervous glance at the dark, forbidding forest and felt her heart sink.

"Come on, Ellen," said Davie.

"Not her." Ushig turned back and held up a hand. "She is not here at my invitation."

"Why *are* we here?" Ellen was determined to stand her ground. She would not let Ushig treat her like some piece of useless luggage.

Ushig didn't even bother to look at her, let alone speak. "Come, Davie," he said.

Davie frowned. "If she's not coming, then neither am I." He shot Ellen a worried look. "She shouldn't be here. But she is. And I have to take care of her."

"Why do you concern yourself with her?" Ushig seemed genuinely puzzled.

Davie clamped his lips together in a way Ellen knew very well. There was no shifting him when he had that look on his face.

"It is wiser if she remains here," insisted Ushig.

The two boys stared at each other. Slowly, Davie folded his arms.

"Bring her, then, if you wish," Ushig turned away, "but I fear you will regret it."

With another apprehensive glance towards the trees, Ellen hurried after them, afraid that he might change his mind. Even Ushig's company was better than being left on this deserted shore with no way of finding her way home. At least the disagreement proved one thing. The old, familiar Davie was still there, the one who looked out for his sister, the one who was convinced that she didn't know how to look after herself.

To Ellen's relief, Ushig did not move towards the forest. Instead, he turned to follow the line of the shore.

"I was right, wasn't I?" Davie fell into step alongside Ellen. "He promised he wouldn't hurt me and he hasn't."

Ellen could not deny it. She couldn't work out why they were here and not at the bottom of the canal, drowning beneath the weight of all that filthy water. She fingered the stone round her neck. The charm had not been strong enough to prevent Ushig from bringing them here, but maybe it *had* protected them a little.

"Why did you come with him, Davie?"

"I wanted to see this," said Davie, "but don't worry," he started walking faster as he saw Ushig moving further away, "I'll make sure you get home again."

Ellen clenched her fists, suddenly terribly angry with her brother. "You don't care about anything, do you Davie? Not about me — or anything except following Ushig. How do you think Mum and Dad are feeling right now?" She realized she was shouting and clamped her lips together, afraid to say more, knowing that it wasn't a good idea to make her brother angry.

It was pointless anyway. The Peerie Folk could make you blind to the truth, could even make things seem other than they were — straw could turn into gold, ancient hags into beautiful young women. Danger could be made to seem like fun. Davie trusted Ushig and she would have to wait until something happened to change his mind.

The relief she felt when Davie refused to leave her behind began to fade and soon Ellen was focused only on the struggle to keep up with him and Ushig. They trudged on for what felt like hours, though the dim grey light never changed. When she stopped to catch her breath, and looked back to see how far they had come, she gasped in surprise. The sand behind her was smooth, as though it had just been washed by the tide.

"Look, Davie," she called. "No footprints!"

Davie frowned and turned back. His frown changed from annoyance to fascination as he watched the sand flow into the dents their feet had left, the holes gradually filling up until there was no sign that anyone had passed this way.

He laughed. "Looks like someone's tidying up behind us."

There was another odd thing. On Aldhammer shore, the pockets of sand between the rocks were ribbed from the water washing over them as the tide moved in and out, but here the surface was smooth and flat. All the time they had been walking, the sea had not moved up or down the beach and there were no piles of seaweed to mark the tide line.

She opened her mouth to tell Davie, but he grabbed hold of her arm before she could speak.

"Something's coming!"

Ushig had stopped a little way ahead. He was watching a small dumpy shape make its way off the rocks. Ellen heard a clattering, like somebody dragging something across stone. As the object moved towards them across the sand, she saw it was a creature about the size of a three-year-old child, covered from head to foot in shells and seaweed. It was the shells banging together that made the clattering noise.

The thing stopped in front of Ushig.

"Ah've been sent tae fetch ye," it said in a low, gravelly voice.

Ushig looked down at it disdainfully. "You have no business with me."

Ellen caught the briefest glimpse of a parrot-like beak and a single eyeball, glaring at Ushig from behind the curtain of seaweed. The eye swivelled round in her direction. It blinked.

"We have no time for this." Ushig jerked his chin at Davie and turned away.

"Aye, ye'll come," it said. "Or ye'll have the seal folk tae answer to."

"I know what you are!" Ellen was delighted to come across something she recognised, no matter how strange. "You're a shellycoat!" Her book said the shellycoat wasn't evil, that it acted from mischief rather than malice.

"And I know what you are," said the shellycoat. "You're a human child. More or less."

It was hard to tell whether it was being rude or just honest. It reached up with knobbly green fingers and patted her jacket. "Odd fur," it said.

Ellen smiled and reached out her own hand, lightly touching the pearls that were threaded through the seaweed. Before she had time to pull away, the shellycoat opened its beak and nipped her finger.

"Ouch!" Ellen snatched it back to see a bright bead of blood swelling on her fingertip.

The creature made a sound like gurgling water. It was laughing. "Got ye there," it said.

Ellen frowned. "I wasn't going to hurt you."

The shellycoat gurgled again. "Maybe not — but I *was* going to hurt you. Keep yer hands off ma pearls."

Ushig made up his mind. "We will come," he said. "But these two are mine."

The single eyeball blinked. "Ye're on the border between the land and the sea," said the shellycoat. "Not a good place tae defy the seal folk."

"These two are nothing to the seal folk," insisted Ushig.

"Aye, well, that's between you and them. "Ah'm only the messenger." The shellycoat gestured towards a jagged outcrop of red sandstone and turned to lead the way. It looked exactly the same from the back as it did from the front.

Chapter 12

Ellen rounded the corner and slammed into Davie, who had stopped right in front of her. She peered over his shoulder and gasped in surprise. The sandy cove beyond was alive with seals. Everywhere she looked, heads popped up out of the sea and there were more, many more, basking on the rocks that reared up out of the still surface of the water.

She laughed in delight as a flurry of seal pups cascaded off the rocks, their vibrant energy oddly out of place in this twilight world, then she stopped abruptly, feeling shy and awkward when every head turned towards her, whiskers twitching.

The seals were not alone. Mixed in among them were people dressed in heavy fur robes. One of them stood up and clambered down from the rocks. Ellen drew a deep breath, her stomach tingling with a mixture of apprehension and anticipation as she recognised the selkie girl from Aldhammer shore.

"That's the girl I told you about," she said to Davie.

He turned to her in surprise.

"See Davie? She was real after all!"

But her brother didn't seem inclined to apologise.

Like Ushig, he was watching closely as the girl walked towards them.

The shellycoat scuttled forward. "I fetched them," it said. "Now ye have to pay."

The girl tossed a small round object in his direction. The shellycoat reached up and caught it with its knobbly fingers. One large, round eyeball emerged from behind the curtain of seaweed and he turned the pearl around, examining it carefully before he gave a satisfied click and tucked it away.

"That's me off then." It cast a quick glance at Ellen. "You humans don't taste very nice, you know," then it scuttled off into a damp crack in the rocks.

Ellen was glad to see it go. Her finger still throbbed from its sharp bite. She turned her attention to the selkie, marvelling at the glossy thickness of the fur round her shoulders. It could never be mistaken for the skin of a dead animal.

"You!" Ushig's pale face darkened with anger. He swung round to Ellen and stared at her for a moment before he turned back to the girl. "It was you, wasn't it? You were the one who told her about the bridle."

The selkie girl tilted her head, a smile tugging the corners of her mouth. "Did you think we would not know you? You cannot hide your nature as easily as that." She turned to Ellen and said, "Welcome, cousin."

Ellen smiled back, tears of relief prickling her eyes at the unexpected appearance of a friendly face. "I got the bridle on," she told the girl. "But Davie took it off."

"You never told me what you were making," Davie said in an accusing tone.

Ellen sighed. "Why would I tell you? All you could think about was the fun you were having with that ... *thing* there." She glanced at Ushig, who stood with his arms folded, staring at her with narrowed eyes as though he was seeing her properly for the first time.

The selkie girl's smile showed two rows of sharp white teeth. "Perhaps I was not so blind as you thought."

"You tricked me well," Ushig said to the selkie. "I cannot deny it. You seemed so very timid." He gave a sharp nod, as though acknowledging a game well played.

The seal girl smiled again. It was comforting to see that she, at least, had no fear of the water wraith when she was here among her own folk.

"Caution is not the same as stupidity." The girl turned from him to Ellen and Davie and gestured towards the cove. "There is someone here who is eager to meet you."

The children followed her through the gap in the rock on to a wide expanse of sand. Ellen glanced back to see that Ushig remained behind. He stood just inside the gap, arms folded, a grim look on his face. A wave of hope surged through her. Here at last was a chance not just to speak to Davie on her own, but maybe to find people who could help her.

At the far end of the cove, Ellen saw a woman leaning back against a boulder. Her face was wrinkled, and the hair hanging loose around her shoulders was more grey than brown, but her eyes sparkled with lively interest as she watched them cross the sand towards her.

Davie spoke quietly in Ellen's ear. "What did she mean when she called you cousin?"

"I don't know, Davie." A sudden wild thought popped into her head and she felt her heart beat faster. "But I think maybe we're about to find out."

The seal girl stopped a little distance from the woman. "I see you, Aisil," she said.

The woman nodded. "I see you, Skarra. And I see the ones you bring."

She settled down on the sand and gestured for the children to join her. Ellen knelt down and after a brief pause, Davie followed her lead, a puzzled frown on his face.

Skarra nodded at Ellen and Davie, then she leaped up on to a spur of rock and ran lightly across its jagged surface. When she reached the water she paused for a moment, then she bent her knees and dived. As her body fell towards the sea, Ellen saw the pelt on her shoulders spread like the living thing it was, until it covered her body from head to foot. The girl vanished beneath the water and seconds later, a seal head bobbed up to look at them for a moment, before it sped off to join the others.

Ellen turned back to the woman, who sat watching her, a small smile tugging the corners of her mouth.

"It is a sight, is it not? To see a selkie take to the sea. There are very few human folk who witness such a thing. And fewer still, I think, have ever seen the selkie host gathered together in one place."

Ellen smiled in return, but Davie shifted restlessly and sighed. He turned and looked at Ushig, waiting beside the rocks.

"I'm Ellen," she said, "and this is my brother Davie." She wasn't worried about giving this woman her real name, even though her book warned against it. She knew for certain that it would not harm her here.

Davie ignored the old woman and leaned over to whisper in his sister's ear. "Ellen," he said. "We can't stay here. We have to go. Ushig is waiting."

"Don't be so rude, Davie." Ellen felt her cheeks growing hot with embarrassment. "Ushig can wait."

Wishing she could explain that her brother wasn't normally this unpleasant, Ellen turned away. Only then did she notice that every creature on the rocks, seal and human, had their eyes fixed on her and her brother. She was relieved to see that their gaze was warm and welcoming, not hostile.

She looked back at Davie, who seemed to have forgotten that his reason for coming here was to meet the inhabitants of this world, like the seal folk. He was still looking at Ushig. Ellen blinked at the realization that the selkie didn't feel other-worldly to her. They felt *right*.

"Why are you in such a hurry Davie?" she demanded.

He didn't answer. Ellen jabbed him in the ribs and he turned back to face the old woman, still flicking glances over his shoulder.

The woman didn't seem to be bothered by Davie's behaviour. She smiled at them both and said, "There is no need for an introduction. I know who you are." Then she leaned forward and looked searchingly into both their faces. "But do you know who I am?"

Davie looked at her in surprise and shook his head. Ellen stared at the heart-shaped, wrinkled face with its familiar dark brown eyes. It was like looking through a window at her own far distant future.

"Yes." She spoke with absolute certainty. There was no doubt in her mind. The words she used were oddly formal but somehow they felt exactly right. "You are Aisil, the selkie. And you are my mother's mother."

Chapter 13

Davie let out a gasp of surprise. Aisil leaned forward and laid a webbed hand on his knee. "Marian has told me a lot about you, Davie, and I have seen you from time to time, walking on the shore with your sister."

"But ... Grannie drowned," said Davie. "A long time before we were born. Mum told me."

The woman laughed. "A selkie cannot drown," she said.

"Marian knows, doesn't she?" Ellen understood now why her aunt stayed close to Aldhammer and why she walked the shore, even in the wildest weather. It wasn't just for work, or pleasure. It was to spend time with her mother, whose true home was the sea.

Aisil nodded. "Marian comes to me." A shadow darkened her face. "But not my eldest. Not my Laura."

"Mum never goes near Aldhammer if she can help it," said Davie.

Ellen could have kicked him when she saw the shadow deepen on Aisil's face.

Davie saw it for himself and he flushed. "I think we could get Mum to Aldhammer and down to the shore. Don't you, Ellen?"

He took his eyes off this amazing grandmother

to glance at his sister and Ellen felt a sudden wave of mingled affection and relief. The real Davie was still there, locked away behind the manic obsession that had taken such a hold of him. It gave her renewed hope.

"I think so," she agreed, "but I don't know if she would believe us if we told her about you."

"I think Laura already knows," said Aisil, "though she may pretend she does not. She has been angry with me for a long time. She blames me for leaving her and Marian."

Ellen wasn't so sure that Aisil was right. She opened her mouth to say so, but Davie spoke first.

"Well," he pointed out, "you *did* leave her."

Ellen could have kicked him all over again but Aisil only nodded. "Yes, I did. But I had no choice." She rose to her feet and began to pace up and down. Ellen saw that her toes as well as her fingers were webbed. Fascinated, she watched the grains of sand fill the spaces where Aisil walked.

"It was for love of me that your grandfather stole my fur and kept it hidden so I could not return to the sea."

Aisil's voice grew low and sad. Ellen could see how hard it was for her to revisit such painful memories.

"It is not easy for a selkie to live upon the land," said Aisil. "The air is thin, not like the water, and hands and feet are heavy, clumsy tools."

"Did Grandad not give you back your seal skin?" Ellen found it hard to believe that the kind, gentle man she remembered could have been so cruel.

Aisil looked at Ellen. "He was a good man, your grandfather, but love made him selfish. He was sorry for it soon enough. In the end, he only kept my skin because he did not want his children to lose their mother." Her eyes swelled with tears. "But I had other children, before my human daughters. Night after night I heard them cry for me as I sat on the shore." She sank back down on the sand, her mind clearly fixed on a time long ago, when she had been forced to make an impossible choice. "It was Marian who found it. She knew that I would die for want of the sea and so she let me come home."

"Why did she let Mum think you were dead?" Ellen knew that one way or another, she would have found a way to get Davie down to the shore to meet his mother.

Aisil stared out over the sea, then looked back at Ellen. "She tried, but Laura would not listen. It was Laura who told her father that Marian needed help. He took her to a doctor." She paused, searching for the right words. "A doctor of the mind."

"You mean a psychiatrist?" It seemed that Davie was listening after all, even if most of his attention remained on the distant shape lurking beside the rocks.

"Yes." Aisil frowned. "It took Marian a long time to learn to speak the words they wanted to hear." She smiled and shook her head. "Skarra really is your cousin, you know. My son's daughter. We are your family."

Ellen couldn't prevent the huge grin that spread

itself across her face. It vanished when she caught sight of Ushig shifting restlessly in the shadows.

"We have to go," said Davie. He stood up. "Come on, Ellen."

"But we only just got here!" Ellen was ready to protest further but Aisil laid a hand on her arm.

"Let him go, child," she said. "He cannot help himself."

"Yes I can," said Davie hotly, "but I promised I would go with him and I have to keep my promise. We'll come back," he added with a grin. "That's another promise!" Already he was moving away.

"He has no choice," said Aisil. "He has given himself into the power of the wraith." She sighed. "Why did you not bridle the beast? I sent Skarra with word of what to do."

"I tried," said Ellen. "But Davie threw it off." Her only weapon was a whole world away, trampled into the mud beside the canal. She looked at her grandmother with fear in her eyes. "What does Ushig want with us?"

"I do not know," said Aisil. "I only know that the Queen gave Ushig the power to open a gate and it will be for no good purpose that he has brought your brother here."

"Who *is* this Queen?" Ellen was absolutely positive that Robert Kirk had never mentioned her.

Aisil sighed. "She rules the land. This world is hers, except for a few places, here and there."

She touched Ellen lightly on one arm and Ellen felt warmth flow from her grandmother's hand. "Ushig thought to rid himself of you when he plunged into the water, but you had a secret that kept you safe."

Ellen reached for the stone around her neck but Aisil shook her head.

"It was not the stone. It was because of the selkie blood that flows in your veins. I told you, Ellen. A selkie cannot drown."

Ellen felt a small glow of pleasure that she had inherited something from her selkie grandmother. "It must be wonderful to swim like a selkie."

Aisil stared at her thoughtfully. "The blood is strong in you." Her glance flicked towards Davie, who was now back at Ushig's side. "But your brother has chosen a different path. He thinks he is taking care of you. He is wrong. It is you who see the danger and you who found the courage to follow him."

"It was an accident really. I didn't mean to come." Ellen felt uncomfortable about taking credit for the thoughtless impulse that had sent her tumbling into the canal.

"You were brave enough to make the bridle and use it," said Aisil. She looked back at Davie. "I do not think your brother can help himself."

"But why not?" Ellen's voice rose in anger and frustration. "Why can't he see what Ushig really is?"

"It is not Davie's fault," insisted Aisil. "Ushig has woven a glamour to capture his heart and mind. He no longer sees the truth."

Ellen stared at her grandmother. "Davie's under a spell?"

Aisil nodded.

"It's just like Robert Kirk," said Ellen thoughtfully.

Aisil's eyebrows lifted in surprise. "You have read his book?"

"Aunt Marian gave it to me." Ellen frowned in concentration, struggling to remember. At the beginning of the book, after the shadow woman set him free, Robert Kirk realized that the food in his bowl was nothing more than a handful of shrivelled mushrooms, black with mould. Then the walls around him tore like paper and he found himself sitting on a rock in a dank and gloomy cavern, lit only by a single candle in the shadow's hand. The shadow had taken pity on him and lifted the spell, but try as she might, Ellen could not remember reading anything about how it was done.

She pictured the page in her head and suddenly, she had it. "It was the rhyme! Remember the rhyme at the top of the page? That's got to be it!" Her heart lifted and she felt a sudden surge of excitement. "It was something to do with blood ... and darkness ..." she laid a hand on her grandmother's arm and looked hopefully at Aisil, but the old woman was shaking her head.

"I cannot help you, Ellen."

"Why not?" Ellen couldn't believe it. This was her one chance to save Davie and it seemed as though her grandmother wasn't even willing to try and help her.

Aisil took Ellen's hand and gently stroked her fingers. "That book was a comfort to me because it showed me pictures of the world I had lost. But the words meant nothing. I cannot read, Ellen."

Ellen's shoulders slumped in disappointment. She had read it too quickly, eager to find out what happened next, especially at the beginning. She would not be able to remember it on her own.

Aisil's eyes clouded with worry as she watched Ellen struggle to deal with her disappointment. "The water wraith is sly — and clever. I fear for you if you try to deal with him alone. You are so very young." She rose to her feet and reached out a hand. "Come with me. There is someone I think you should meet."

Chapter 14

Mystified, Ellen followed Aisil deeper into the rocks. They emerged in a small sandy cove where seal pups slid eagerly in and out among the waves. When Aisil turned away from the water, Ellen was surprised by how hard it was to pull free from the almost irresistible urge to join them as she followed Aisil across the cove to where a hunched figure sat shrouded in a hooded cloak, watching over the pups.

The face that looked up at her was one Ellen had never seen before. She stared, puzzled, at his faded blue eyes and his flowing white beard.

"The seal folk took him home," said Aisil. "That was how we first came to the village of Aldhammer." Her soft voice trembled slightly. "Some of us did not learn its dangers until it was too late."

Ellen knew Aisil was talking about herself, but she had eyes only for the old man who stared at her in obvious surprise.

"A human child!" He grinned in delight, his face splitting into a thousand wrinkles.

"He came back to us in the end," said Aisil. "He was a stranger in his own world, for no one believed the things he had seen and done."

The old man clasped his hands together as he smiled up at Ellen. "This world was never meant for such as you and I, but all the same, it gladdens my heart to see a human child once more."

Ellen blinked in disbelief. It should have been impossible, but there was only one person this could possibly be. "I know who you are! You're Rob ..."

The smile disappeared and he raised his hand in warning. "Do not speak that name here!"

"When he was a child," said Aisil, "he fell into a stream and nearly drowned. His brothers and sisters called him 'Glub', for that was the noise he made when they pulled him out." She laughed. "The Queen never had a true name to call him by." Kneeling on the sand, she gestured for Ellen to do the same.

"Glub," Aisil said softly, "this child's brother is trapped by a glamour, spun by a servant of the Queen."

A hunted look appeared in his eyes. "I cannot help, Aisil. Do not ask me. If I act against her, she will know." His voice had risen to a weedy wail. "She will find me ..."

"But it's important!" The words burst from Ellen's lips, her fear for her brother obliterating any sympathy she felt for this tired old man.

"Hush, Ellen." Aisil kept her eyes on Robert Kirk's face. "The child is here for her brother's sake, but that is not why I brought her to you. I thought you would like to know that your book did make a difference after all."

"My book?" He looked from Aisil to Ellen in

surprise. "But no one believed me. They thought I made it up."

"I believed you," said Ellen, though honesty compelled her to add, "not at first, maybe, but in the end I did. You helped me, just like the shadow woman helped you."

The old man's gaze drifted away. "She was human once, you know. She was a farmer's wife. I pleaded with her but she would not return to a world where she was long forgotten." A tear glistened in his eye. "She will have faded to nothing by now."

Ellen opened her mouth, but shut it again as Aisil laid a warning hand on her arm.

"She set you free, didn't she? There was a rhyme she spoke to break the spell."

He shook his head and Ellen felt tears cloud her own eyes at the unbearable thought that her hopes had come to nothing. But the tears melted away when he said, "It wasn't a rhyme. It was a riddle."

He thought for a moment, then gathered his cloak more tightly round his body and began to speak.

"I run in darkness,
Salt like the sea.
Death will come quickly,
If I break free."

He clapped his hands together, clearly delighted with himself, then he frowned. Ellen's hopes crashed again when he added, "I never did work out what it meant."

She could not keep silent any longer. "But you were there! You must remember!"

He studied her face for a moment, then he

said, "I'm sorry, child. I heard the words, but the glamour bound me too deeply to see how she used them." His blue eyes grew misty with memory. "My shadow freed me with her clear sight and her loving heart. I hope you can do the same for your brother."

"We must go now, Ellen," said Aisil. "Davie is waiting."

Ellen glanced back once as she followed her grandmother. Despite her worries, she smiled at the sight of the old man sitting beneath a pearl grey sky, surrounded by creatures from another world. It was good to know that Robert Kirk had found a place for himself among the selkie.

A sudden impulse sent her running back. She knelt down in front of him. "Thank you for the book. It helped me so very much."

The old man nodded. "Maybe I wrote it just for you," he said with an impish grin, before his eyes wandered back to the seal pups in the water.

"Give it time," said Aisil as they walked away. "It will come to you eventually and you will free your brother of the glamour that dazzles him."

But there wasn't any time. They came out into the bay to see Davie standing at the opposite end. When he caught sight of Ellen he frowned ferociously and lifted his arm in an impatient gesture. She could almost feel his annoyance from here.

Aisil took a deep breath. "Ellen," she said, "would you like to stay with me? At least you would be safe while we searched for some way to help your brother."

Ellen blinked in surprise at this unexpected

offer. It would be wonderful to stay here, to be comforted by her grandmother, free of Ushig's brooding presence.

"Can't you make Davie stay here too?" But she could already see the answer in those sorrowful brown eyes.

"Not your brother. I cannot hold him here. He came willingly with Ushig and he is his creature now. But I can keep you safe, if you wish it."

Ellen shook her head slowly. It wouldn't work. She would worry even more, wondering what was happening to Davie. Suddenly, like an unstoppable tidal wave, the thing she had tried so hard to forget reared up and overwhelmed her.

"It's all my fault!" Hot tears rose in her eyes and ran down her face. "I said the rhyme. The calling rhyme! I'm the one who brought Ushig!"

"No, child." Aisil leaned forward and took Ellen's hands in hers. "It was an accident. You might as well blame Marian for teaching you the rhyme in the first place. She did mean for you to use it, you know. Although not for that purpose."

Aisil's webbed fingers felt warm and comforting. Ellen blinked at her grandmother through her tears. "To call you?"

The old woman nodded. She let go of Ellen's hands and leaned back against the rock, studying her carefully. "Marian thought you would be able to accept what I am."

Ellen wiped her face on her sleeve. "So that's why she gave me the book." Calmer now, she frowned at her grandmother. "Why did Ushig choose Davie when I was the one who called him?

Was it just an accident that Davie climbed on his back instead of me?"

"You are right," said Aisil. "That is odd. Davie is older and stronger than you." Her piercing eyes searched Ellen's face. "But there are other kinds of strength, Ellen."

"I can't stay here," said Ellen with deep regret. "I have to go." There was no contest really. And not just because of her brother.

Aisil understood. "For your mother's sake and your father's, you must help him find his way home."

"I can come back, though," Ellen said eagerly. "Now I know, I can come back here again."

Aisil shook her head. "The selkie can move from world to world. But only the Queen can open a gate for others. Perhaps I can see you when I visit Marian, but I will not risk the land for long."

Ellen was disappointed but she couldn't blame her — not after all those years a prisoner in Aldhammer, longing for her home in the sea. "I will go with my brother," she repeated.

Aisil reached over and wrapped her arms round her granddaughter. Ellen clung tightly, breathing in the warm salt smell of the sealskin round Aisil's shoulders before she finally let go. In silence, Aisil watched Ellen trudge across the sand towards Ushig and Davie.

"Are you ready, then?" Davie's voice was eager.

Ellen turned to exchange a final wave and spotted the shellycoat lurking in the shadows between the rocks. Reaching out, she took hold of a piece of the crinkly seaweed dangling from its head and tugged hard. It made an angry sound, like waves hissing on shingle.

"Now we're even," said Ellen, and she laughed, grateful for something to take her mind off her worries.

The shellycoat tilted its upper body and she glimpsed the beady eye peering at her. "Aye," it said. "You're her granddaughter all right."

Chapter 15

"You remain with us?" Ushig raised an eyebrow when he saw Ellen emerge from the space between the rocks. "But your brother tells me you have found your grandmother."

He said the last word carefully, concentrating on getting it right. Ushig thought he understood about family, but he didn't. Not if he thought you could exchange one family member with another, like a set of identical dolls.

"Ushig's right, Ellen." Davie looked back at the seal folk, then at his sister. A smile flickered across his face and for a moment she thought he had changed his mind about going with Ushig.

"It seems safe here," he said. "Safer than the forest." He turned to Ushig. "When we come back, we'll take her home with us."

Ellen wanted to tell him it was more a question of *if* they went home again, not when, but she knew now there was no point in arguing with him. "As long as you have Davie," she said to Ushig, "I have to follow."

"But Davie does not want you," Ushig pointed out.

"Davie doesn't know what he wants!"

Her brother sighed and draped one arm across

her shoulder. "Don't sulk, Ellen. Ushig hasn't *got* me — he asked if I wanted an adventure and I said yes." He swung her round and pointed to the tree line. "Look," he said eagerly. "That's where I'm going. To meet the ruler of the world!"

"The Queen can calm the waters, but she does not rule the people of the sea."

Ellen whirled round. Skarra stood behind her, the sealskin slung across one shoulder like a short tunic.

"Aisil did not ask," she said, "but I know it will comfort her if I am with you."

Ushig laughed. "You are better here, I think. The forest is not meant for your kind."

Skarra stared at him. "I am family too."

Ushig raised an eyebrow. "Family again?" Then he shrugged. "Do as you will."

When he turned to Davie, his voice changed. It sounded younger, more eager. "Let's go! We've wasted enough time here already!"

Davie set off, chatting enthusiastically to Ushig while Ellen and Skarra followed more slowly. From time to time the wraith's eyes drifted back towards them. It seemed as though he still could not grasp why Ellen was so determined to stay with her brother.

From somewhere deep within the forest she heard a wail of despair, rising swiftly to a crescendo of anguished sobbing. Ellen's steps faltered but Skarra laid a comforting hand on her arm.

Ushig glanced back. "The banshee cannot harm you. Not while we are travelling the Royal Road on the Queen's business."

Ellen was sure his reassuring words were not for her sake. He was probably worried that if Ellen stopped, then Davie might too.

Her brother grinned cheerfully. "Come on then, if you're coming. Best foot forward!"

Ellen felt a shiver of apprehension as she watched him step into the darkness beneath the trees.

"Ushig is right, Ellen," said Skarra. "The road is safe. No one on the Queen's business will come to harm."

Ellen took one last regretful look at the shore before she walked on. "What happens if you're not on the Queen's business?"

"Then the road leads to places that no one would willingly choose to go," said Skarra, falling into step beside her.

Ellen felt her feet sink into a dense carpet of moss, as short as a well-kept lawn. "But how would the Queen know? She's a long way from here, isn't she?" She didn't really care about the answer. She just wanted to take her mind off her fears.

Skarra shrugged. "The Queen is part of the land. Perhaps she feels the intentions of those who tread its ways."

Ellen could put it off no longer. There was only one way. Forward. Together, the girls set off along the path, an emerald green thread leading deeper into the dim interior of the wood. On either side, the tree branches stopped abruptly, as though someone had been at work with an electric hedge-trimmer. Below the trees, a mass of jagged brambles formed an impenetrable wall of dense undergrowth.

Ellen found this woodland oddly familiar, maybe because Robert Kirk had travelled this way, though he had been going in the opposite direction, towards the sea. She thought of his description of stumbling through these woods, tormented by the Ghillie Dhu, the secretive inhabitants of the birch wood, of how he was tricked and led astray by boggarts, then rescued by Gruach, the Herdswoman, who gathers up those who are lost or gone astray. Gruach fed him, cared for him and led him at last to the sea.

Ellen sighed. If only Gruach would appear right now. But she didn't sound like the kind of person who would seek out those who travelled with a water wraith for company.

Skarra reached out her hand and Ellen took it. The other girl's webbed fingers felt slightly odd, but Ellen was comforted by the knowledge that she did not have to do this alone.

Her cousin also seemed to welcome the contact. For her, too, these woods must be a strange, unknown place. "Did Glub have anything useful to offer? He is an old man, but he knows much."

Ellen sighed. "He gave me a riddle, but I can't make any sense of it."

"Perhaps we can unravel it together. Let me hear it."

Frowning in concentration, Ellen repeated the words, knowing it was important to get it exactly right. "He said ... 'I run in darkness, salt like the sea. Death will come swiftly, if I break free.'"

She looked hopefully at Skarra, but her cousin shook her head, mystified. They walked on, each one struggling to come up with answers but finding only questions. What was it that ran in darkness? An underground river? But how would that bring death? And how could it be salt like the sea?

At last, her head spinning, Ellen gave up and once again turned her attention to the road they walked.

The forest was full of creatures —the sobs of the banshee and the tempting melody from the hidden piper were proof of that — but there was no birdsong, not even the sound of leaves rustling in the wind. No sunlight filtered down to the forest floor, although there was enough light to see by: a pearly glow that hovered around Ellen and Skarra like a faint grey mist.

Anxious to break the oppressive silence, Ellen turned to her newfound cousin. "I'm glad you're here."

Skarra nodded. "I will stay with you as long as I can." She spoke quietly, as though she, too, found it hard to disturb the silence. "But I must warn you, Ellen. Ushig is right. I cannot go far from the sea."

The mossy carpet began to grow soggy underfoot. Ellen's feet sank a little with every step she took. Clumps of red and white toadstools lurked beneath the bushes at the side of the path. They reminded her of a picture that once hung on her bedroom wall. There had been a tiny fairy peeping out of a doorway in the stem. In this place, she knew that whatever lurked inside such a poisonous growth would bring not good dreams, but nightmares.

The ground grew drier underfoot as the road began to climb. The toadstools disappeared. Something rustled in the trees and she looked up to see a pair of yellow eyes staring down at her. There was a snigger, followed by a soft giggle from the other side of the path. Ellen moved closer to Skarra.

They were climbing away from the sea, heading inland, but it was almost impossible to guess how far they had travelled. The forest enclosed her like a soft green blanket. Without the sun, time had no meaning, but Ellen thought they must have been walking for hours. Davie and Ushig strode ahead, shoulder to shoulder, without a backward glance. Ellen tried to walk faster but already she was finding it hard to keep up.

She waded across a small stream and felt a powerful urge to reach down and dip her fingers in the water that swirled about her ankles. For a brief moment she found herself wondering if it was because the water reminded her of the safe haven offered by the seal folk. The thought faded away, driven from her head by the concentration required to put one foot in front of the other. Grateful for Skarra's steadying hand, she plodded on, her legs aching more with every dip they descended and every hill they climbed. In spite of her efforts to struggle on, she knew she was falling further and further behind.

She stopped and looked back. Through a break in the trees she caught a glimpse of the land falling away towards the shoreline. There was no town and no railway line, but the view looked oddly familiar, like a time-lapse photograph, with the past lying over the present. It was a vision of her own world, before people arrived to cut down the trees and turn the forest into fields.

When she turned back to the path she saw Davie walking towards her, a long-suffering look on his face. Ushig was waiting a little further ahead, at yet another of those endless twists and turns.

"You have to keep up," said Davie. "Ushig says this place can be dangerous."

"Your sister is here because of you," Skarra reminded him sharply.

"I'm doing my best." Ellen found herself wishing she could explain to Skarra that the real Davie was much nicer than this. "Where are we going anyway?" She didn't expect a sensible answer. She just wanted a chance to get her breath back.

"Ushig says there's a place up ahead where we can get a good view of everything," said Davie. Dark shadows ringed his eyes, but he was jiggling from foot to foot, unable to control his restless need to move on.

"What makes you think it'll look any different from this?" She spun round again, pointing at the track behind them. It looked exactly the same as it did in front, except for a little puff of wind dancing across the moss like a miniature storm. Ellen rubbed her eyes. Had she really seen tiny figures spinning in and out of the dust?

"The Sluach." Ushig's voice whispered in her ear and she jumped. She hadn't heard him coming.

"They are spirits who travel on the wind," he said, "and they are terrible thieves."

"I know what they are," she snapped. "I've read about them."

Something tugged at her hair. She reached up to slap it away, then turned to glare at Ushig.

"Not me." He held up both hands and grinned at her.

She frowned and looked away.

"We are safe enough," Ushig went on. "But we cannot linger."

They set off once more, Skarra and Ellen linking arms to help each other along. From time to time, other paths joined with theirs and Ellen glanced eagerly down each one, hoping to see something other than trees and bushes, but when at last she did, she only walked faster, anxious to put some space between herself and that deep, dark pool surrounded by red and blue and purple lupins.

Gradually, the trees began to thin and the air grew lighter. She spotted movement in the bushes and stopped, her heart thumping, but it was only a deer, crashing its way through the undergrowth. She smiled at the sight of its white tail bobbing into the distance before she remembered that in this place, things were not always what they seemed.

Trees gave way to patches of grass and outcrops of bare rock. Ellen hauled herself along, Skarra beside her, both girls now leaning on each other for support. At last, with a tremendous sense of relief, she heard Davie calling out to her, his voice high with excitement.

"Ellen! Hurry up! I know where we are!"

Chapter 16

"Look!" Davie pointed across the forest at the grey expanse of the sea. "That's where Aldhammer should be. This world is the same as our own — more or less," he added as Ellen opened her mouth to tell him she had worked that out for herself.

"This is definitely the top of Rigley Hill. And *that's* where we're going." He pointed to a huge, flat-topped hill rising out of the surrounding forest. "Traprain Law!"

Ellen's heart sank as she stared at the massive rock dominating the inland horizon. They had gone there one day with Aunt Marian. It had only taken about half an hour in the car. But this time there was no car.

"It's awfully far away, Davie," she said. Her legs wobbled and she thumped down on to the ground beside Skarra.

Ushig looked at her with annoyance, but Davie said, "I need a rest too," and flopped down on the springy turf. With a dark look at all three, Ushig walked off and stood with his back to them, staring across the forest towards Traprain Law.

Ellen had no idea how long it had been since she woke to find herself on the shore. They had certainly travelled a long way — far enough for the sea to be no more than a grey expanse in the distance. It was odd that she didn't feel hungry. It was even stranger that she wasn't thirsty either. How long was it since any food or drink had passed her lips?

"This world seems to be outside of time, somehow," she said to Davie, struggling to find the right words to explain what she was thinking. "As though nothing ever changes."

"You mean no sunrise, or sunset?" said Davie. "Ushig says the Queen holds the light, but I'm not sure what he means." He looked down at Skarra, who was curled up on the ground, white-faced and panting for breath. A worried frown crinkled his forehead. "Are you all right?"

Ellen was glad to see the real Davie surface again, even if it was only for a moment. It gave her hope that the change in him was only temporary.

"I thought I would be a help to you," Skarra looked up at Ellen, "but I am only a burden now."

"No, you're not," said Ellen, though she knew it was true. Skarra's helping hand had become a heavy weight by the time they reached the top of the hill.

Davie turned to Ushig. He had lost interest in Skarra. "If we're moving from one place to another," he asked, "doesn't that make the world change?"

Ushig moved closer and sat down. "All things change in the end."

"Like if there's a storm?" Davie pointed to a fallen tree a little way down the hill.

"Ah, well," Ushig looked hard at the tree. "Storms can topple trees, but who directs the storm?"

"Storms just happen," said Ellen.

Ushig looked at her, saying nothing. Ellen was too tired to pursue it. She lay back and closed her eyes, hoping the hard ground beneath her might iron itself out into something more comfortable, while her mind worried away at Robert Kirk's riddle.

"If nothing changes, then how are we supposed to get where we're going?" she heard Davie ask Ushig.

"We move as we are bid," came the mysterious answer.

"Well, can't you magic up some faster way of moving then?"

"I can," said Ushig. "If you will ride the wraith."

"No!" Ellen sat up, glared at both of them, then lay down again. If she didn't rest, she knew she would never be able to continue, but her brain refused to slow down, her thoughts darting this way and that, thinking of this strange world, of her grandmother and the selkie blood that flowed in her veins. But those were merely distractions from the worry that dominated everything else.

She *had* to free her brother from the glamour that blinded him to the truth. But no matter how hard she struggled to understand the riddle, she could think of nothing that came even close to an answer.

It was almost a relief when Davie nudged her with his toe and reached down a helping hand. "We really need to get going."

She climbed stiffly to her feet. With one last

glance at the naked hilltop that marked the Law,
she followed Davie and the wraith along the trail
and back into the forest. She refused to think
about what might be waiting for them until they
finally arrived.

Footsore and weary, Ellen and Skarra moved
doggedly forward. Ellen had no energy left to look
around her. There was no point in looking anyway.
All she could see were the trees and the endless
green path.

A short while later, Skarra staggered across
another little stream, tripped over her own feet
and thudded down on to the soft moss. Davie
turned to look, then retraced his steps.

He stared at Skarra for a moment then glanced
at Ellen and said, "We'll stop here for a while."

Ellen nodded. She was too tired to speak.
Together, she and Davie took hold of Skarra and
half dragged, half carried her a little further up
the road where she leaned back against a lichen-
covered rock. Ellen sank down gratefully beside
her cousin.

"Let them stay there," Ushig called to Davie.

"I'm not going without my sister." Davie's face
had a set, stubborn look.

Ushig walked slowly back. "You will not leave
her?"

Davie shook his head. "Maybe we could have
something to eat," he suggested. "We could light a
fire — there's plenty of dead wood." He pointed to
an ancient tree, its branches littering the ground
beside the track.

"No fires." Skarra and Ushig spoke in unison.

They looked at each other and exchanged a grudging smile.

"Fire attracts things," said Ushig. "And the wood you see is not yours to burn." He looked around. "Wait here. I will see what I can find for you to eat."

He pushed his way through the dense wall of bushes with surprising ease and disappeared into the trees. Ellen laid a hand on her brother's arm.

"Davie, we mustn't eat anything."

For what felt like the hundredth time, Ellen heard him sigh.

"Why not?"

"I don't think the food here will be good for us. My book says, if you eat food, then you might never get home."

"You're probably right," said Davie. "Alien food could be poisonous. I'm not hungry anyway," he ended, on a note of surprise.

Ellen felt her irritation rising. Davie still thought he was some sort of galactic hero, bravely searching out new worlds. She swallowed her annoyance and smiled up at him. It wasn't her brother's fault. He was trapped by the glamour Ushig had woven around him.

"Davie," she said. "Do you know where we're going?"

"I told you," said Davie. "We're going to Traprain Law." He picked a stem of grass and put it to his lips, then he caught his sister's eye and threw it away.

"Yes ... but *why* are we going to the Law?"

"Ushig wants me to meet the Queen. That's why

we're on the Royal Road. We have to meet her on
Traprain Law."

"Is that why he's in such a hurry?" Ellen moved a
little closer to her brother and lowered her voice in
case Ushig was somewhere nearby. "He didn't want
us to spend any time with the seal folk. Maybe there
were things he didn't want them to tell us."

Davie leaned back against the rock. His eyes
flickered towards Skarra and away. "Ellen, you've
got it wrong. The seal folk don't like the Queen.
They would have stopped us coming if they could
and Ushig is in a hurry for our sake. The longer we
take, the more creatures will follow us. They can
smell us." For once, he looked uneasy.

But Ellen didn't notice. "Davie!" She clutched
his arm. "Look!"

He followed her pointing finger back the way
they had come. A woman was crouched beside
the stream. She was dressed all in grey, in an old-
fashioned skirt that billowed about her as she bent
to swirl a rag to and fro in the water. She lifted
it up in the air where it hung, dripping, as she
turned her head towards them. Ellen shivered at
the sight of that wrinkled, skull-like face.

"All right, Ellen," Davie said with exaggerated
patience. "What does your book tell us about her?"

But it was Skarra who answered. "A shadow
shape of cloud and mist, of gloom and dusk." Her
voice was a hoarse whisper. "She is the Washer at
the Ford."

The old woman looked at them for a long time,
expressionless, then she rose to her feet and
disappeared into the bushes, the dripping rag still

dangling from one hand.

Ellen stared at the empty space where she had stood. "If you see her, something bad is going to happen. Her appearance is a warning of disaster."

Davie wasn't listening. He was looking the other way, waiting for Ushig to come back.

Ellen tried to remember. Did it mean disaster if she didn't heed the warning? Or did it mean there was nothing she could do about it? She rubbed her forehead. It was hard to think. She was so very tired.

Ushig had told them to stay on the trail. Skarra thought that too, but Skarra herself admitted she knew little of this inland world. And Ellen knew she could trust nothing Ushig said. Maybe the old woman was warning them that Ushig was herding them, like sheep, towards whatever it was that he had planned for Davie.

She glanced over at Skarra, but the seal girl's laboured breathing and closed eyes told her that her cousin was beyond offering any help. Slowly, she climbed back on to her feet.

"Where are you going?" Davie looked round.

"I just wondered how she managed to disappear," said Ellen. "I didn't think there was any way through those bushes."

"Don't be long," said Davie. "Ushig will be back any minute."

Ellen retraced her steps. When she walked into the stream she felt a rush of pleasure as it lapped around her legs. She saw a small gap in the bushes on one side and pushed her way through, to find herself knee deep in a pool of water. Right in front of her, a tumbling cascade poured down a flat slab of rock.

She moved forward, peering at the stone behind the waterfall. It was carved with the figure of a woman in a long robe, her hair held back by a round circlet. In one hand she held a staff with the sinuous shape of a snake. Ellen blinked. For a minute she thought the snake had opened one eye to look at her.

"It is a way sign," said Skarra, from behind her. "It tells us we are on the Royal Road."

"Is that all?" Davie pushed his way through behind Skarra. He flicked a look of annoyance at Ellen. "Ushig told us to stay on the track," he reminded her.

Ellen shrugged. There was no point in voicing her suspicions about Ushig. And in spite of his words, she could tell Davie was interested. He clambered on to the bank while Skarra moved to stand beneath the waterfall. She sighed with relief as the water flowed around her. Ellen fought the urge to join her.

Instead, she climbed up towards Davie, but he walked away, his head tilted up to look up at the massive trees surrounding the pool.

After a moment, though, he turned back. "We'd better go and wait for Ushig."

He only took a few steps before he stopped dead. Ellen's heart jumped in her chest as a skeletal figure rose from a hollow in the grass. It must have been hidden there all the time they were looking around.

Ellen let out a gasp of horror as she saw others

emerging from the trees, their eyes fixed on her and Davie. They moved forward with a shambling walk, clawed hands reaching out, their mouths open with eager anticipation.

She knew what they were. Trows. Half-human, half-animal, they fed on meat. Any meat.

Chapter 17

"Run!" Davie waved Ellen back towards the stream.

He jumped at the creature in front of him, knocking it backwards, then ran towards his sister, but the trow leaped up again and Ellen watched, horrified, as it grabbed hold of Davie's arms. She heard him yell out in panic as the trow threw him to the ground and straddled him with its legs.

Ellen ran forward and threw herself on to the creature that held Davie by the throat. With strength fuelled by desperation, she tugged and clawed at the coarse hair on its back, but it was no use. The trow was thin and wiry, but frighteningly strong. It shook Davie from side to side like a rag doll. She dragged at its head, but a triumphant squeal behind her followed by the feel of sharp fingers scrabbling at her clothes told her she had run out of time.

Suddenly the fingers were gone. A trow landed beside her with a bone crunching thump and she saw Skarra fall on top of it. Her cousin's face was no longer human. Instead, Ellen saw the flat bullet-shaped head and fanged jaws of a sea wolf hunting on the land.

Desperately, Ellen hung on to the hank of hair

in her fist while the trow beneath her struggled to sink its sharp teeth into her brother's throat.

A roar of fury filled the glade and from the corner of her eye she saw Ushig emerge from the trees. The berries in his hands scattered into the dirt. His arms lengthened and he fell forward, his head and body growing huge and dark. The great black horse pawed the ground and opened its mouth to scream its rage and contempt into the faces of the slack-jawed trows. It pounded forward into the shambling pack, gripped one in its razor teeth and threw it into the trees, where it thudded against a trunk and slithered to the ground.

"These are mine!" He roared, his eyes snapping. "You will not touch what is mine!" The trows scattered in confusion, all except the one which held Davie. Unwilling to lose its captive, it was dragging him along, with Ellen still clinging to its back. She felt Ushig's hot breath on her neck as he pulled her off and saw hooves like sickle blades flash past her face. There was a scream of agony, and the trow fell to one side, blood welling from a wound on its face.

Ushig spared a glance for Ellen, his eyes filled with murderous rage. "Get back to the road."

Ellen wasted no time. While Ushig raised those lethal hooves once again, she dragged Davie across the grass and into the pool, floundering over the slippery rocks until she reached the gap in the bushes, where she sank down with her brother's head cradled in her lap. His breath came in great shuddering gasps, but she was simply grateful he was still alive.

"Let me take him out of the water."

Ellen looked up to see Skarra, human once more, her mild brown eyes filled with distress. She let her lift Davie, then staggered to her feet with her back to the green road, watching the trows head into the trees, dragging their fallen comrades along with them.

But some were unwilling to give up the fight. One leaped into the air and landed on Ushig's back. It was joined by another ... and then another. The horse body blurred and Ellen glimpsed another shape, scaly and armour plated. She gasped, shocked by the realization that Ushig must be far older than she had imagined him to be: how else could he take the form of a creature not from myths and stories, but from the earliest history of her own planet, when giant reptiles roamed the earth? Nothing was left of them in her own world, only fossilized remains. Here though, they still existed, thanks to the shape-shifting magic of the wraith.

The transformation was still incomplete when the trow on his back grabbed Ushig's mane, forcing back the massive, blunt-nosed head. The mouth roared its fury, revealing razor sharp teeth, but they clashed on nothing as the trow leaned down from above, claws reaching for the exposed throat.

Ushig once more solidified into a coal black horse, his eyes rolling madly, hindquarters scrabbling for balance on the damp and slippery ground.

Ellen dipped her hand in the water and drew out a smooth, round stone. She raised it in the air.

This was the moment she had waited for. Without Ushig, Davie would have no choice but to come with her, back along the green road to the shore and the safety of the sea.

She took a deep breath and drew back her arm, but it was no good. She couldn't do it. The rock flew from her hand, not towards Ushig, but right in the path of the trow clinging to his back, claws upraised, screaming in excitement. The blow knocked it sideways and it fell, dislodging the others. Ushig's hooves scrabbled to find more solid footing, then he turned and galloped towards the road. Bunching his muscles, he took a massive leap, right over Ellen's head, across the bushes and on to the road beyond.

Ellen turned and crawled quickly through the hole, then she dropped to her knees beside Skarra and Davie, horrified by the sight of the blood that seeped through his sleeve and trickled down his arm. She felt sick. This was all her fault. Slowly, Davie's eyes lost their look of blind panic and focused on her face.

"It's all right," she said gently. "We're safe."

His eyelids fluttered and he smiled up at her. "I told you Ushig was my friend," he said. "He saved my life."

A boy again, Ushig stared down at Davie, his face expressionless, then he looked at Ellen. "And you saved mine."

Ellen jumped up and slammed both fists into Ushig's chest, tears of rage and shame making tracks down her grubby face. "What is it you want with us?"

Ushig made no effort to stop the blows. Eventually, she sank back down beside her brother, angrily brushing away the tears. "Why did you bring us here?"

"We came to follow the green road that leads to your heart's desire." The wraith was looking at her tears with interest, as though they were something he had never seen before.

"And what is that, Ushig?" Skarra's chest was heaving with the effort to draw breath. "What is your heart's desire?"

"What else?" Ushig tilted his head to look at Skarra. "I seek only to serve the Queen of the Night."

Ellen frowned. She was absolutely sure that he was not telling the whole truth.

He glanced around, then shrugged. "In any case, what I want does not matter. I am the Queen's loyal servant." He looked down at Ellen as though she were a puzzle he was slowly working out. "When the trows attacked, you were afraid," he said thoughtfully, "but you were alive. I know you felt alive."

He was right. She could not deny it. There had been fear and there had been guilt. Terrible guilt ... but there was excitement too.

"Your sight is true here."

Her fingers strayed to the discarded glasses in her pocket.

"This place is part of you," said Ushig, his voice soft. "I think you belong here, even if Davie does not."

"If he doesn't belong, then let me take him

home," she said quickly.

His friendly tone evaporated. "I cannot."

Skarra leaned up on one elbow. "These are family," she said. "You have no claim on them."

Ushig looked down at her. "I have no choice."

"There is always a choice," said Skarra. "And more than that. You owe a debt to the one who saved you."

Ushig looked away. Skarra turned to Ellen. "You know I can go no further?"

Ellen nodded, unsurprised. Skarra had done her best, but she could not survive for long this far from the sea and Ellen could not go with her. She could not go home without Davie. When she saw his eyes flutter behind his closed lids and his pale, anxious face move from side to side, the guilt she felt was almost too much to bear.

"You will do your best to take care of your brother," said Skarra, "but I must take to the water. It will lead me to the sea. Look for me near water, Ellen."

"I'll miss you, Skarra," whispered Ellen, as she watched the seal girl move slowly down the path and disappear through the gap in the hedge.

Chapter 18

Ushig stared down at Ellen, his brow furrowed. "Your cousin is right," he said at last. "I owe you a debt of honour."

Ellen looked up, hope blossoming in her heart until she saw him shake his head slowly.

"I have no power to send you home."

"But you could let us go back," Ellen knew her chance had finally come. She had to find a way to take advantage of Ushig's uncertainty.

Ushig wasn't listening. "I should have known," he muttered. "She gives you hope, but always there is poison at the heart."

"If we get back to the seal folk," Ellen persisted, "we would be safe ... Skarra said the sea people are not ruled by your Queen."

Ushig's shifted his attention to Davie, who was breathing more normally now, though his eyes were still closed. Then he looked back at Ellen. "I did not bring you here. It has always been your choice to stay, but Davie is different. I cannot let him go. The Wild Hunt must run and the Queen has chosen me. I am her *Teind.*"

"What's that supposed to mean?"

Ushig sighed. "The Queen holds the names of all those who exist within her lands. I am called to her. I must go and where I go, your brother must follow."

"You're just confusing me!" She was sick of secrets, of clues and puzzles and words with half-hidden meanings that told you enough to make you afraid but never enough to make you understand. "Everything you say just mixes things up more! I don't know what a Teind is. I don't know why names matter so much. I don't know *anything*!"

The wraith frowned at her. "If the Queen has your name, it is a chain that binds you to her. She has called me and I cannot refuse to answer. I have been chosen."

"Chosen for what?" demanded Ellen.

But he turned away without answering.

Ellen sank back on her heels. She licked away a trickle of blood from a scratch on the back of her hand.

The salty taste triggered a connection inside her brain. Salt ... like the sea. Exhilaration coursed through her as she realized — she had solved the riddle at last! Blood flowed through darkness when it was inside the body and people died if their blood was spilt. Her excitement wavered a little at the thought that knowing the answer to the riddle still didn't tell her what she had to do. She cast her mind back, trying to remember. Had the old man said anything that might help? He had told her that her clear sight and a loving heart would free Davie. It wasn't much, but she would do her best.

"From me to you," she whispered as she pressed her trembling fingers against the bright red beads, then reached out to lay her hand gently on Davie's closed eyelids.

"Open your eyes, Davie," she whispered. "Open them and see what I see." Hardly daring to hope, she sat back again, watching Davie's eyelids flutter. He stared up at Ushig. Ellen held her breath.

"I'm sorry," he said. "This is as far as we go. Ellen was right. This place is too dangerous. We have to go back."

Ellen felt her shoulders sag with relief. Davie's eyes no longer shone with the manic glitter of his wild enthusiasm. The glamour was gone.

Ushig stared at Davie, his eyebrows drawn down in a puzzled frown. "Davie ..." he said slowly. "Remember — we are going together to meet the Queen."

Davie shook his head. Raising himself on one elbow, he reached out a hand to Ellen. "Help me up," he said. "We're going home."

Ellen jumped up, weariness forgotten, and hauled him to his feet. With the help of the seal folk, she and Davie would find a way back to their own world. She smiled at her brother. All they had to do was reach the sea.

Ushig was watching Ellen, still frowning. "It seems I underestimated you — and the love you have for your brother." His voice was flat, without expression.

Ellen glanced warily in his direction, but he made no move to stop them. Instead, he folded both arms across his chest and watched.

Davie took a few steps forward and came to a sudden stop.

"Ellen ... I can't."

"Yes you can," Ellen said firmly. She linked her arm in his and pulled him along another step. "I'll help you."

"No," said Davie. "I can't. It's like there's a rope that ties me here — to him." He turned and looked at Ushig, his face full of fear. "He has me, Ellen. I can't leave him."

"That's not true," said Ellen. "Not any more."

"Ellen." Davie sagged in her grip. "It's not possible. My legs won't do it. Every step I take, they get heavier and heavier."

"Please, Davie," begged Ellen, "please don't give up." But she only managed to pull him a little further down the path before he stumbled and fell. Ellen's heart sank. If Davie couldn't walk then she was helpless. She couldn't drag him all the way back to the sea. She bowed her head and sat down beside him, defeated.

"We will rest here for a while," said the wraith. "Then I will carry you."

Ellen looked at him with hatred. "Why would I want to climb on your back?"

"What difference does that make now?" asked Ushig. "I am sorry for it, but there is no other way."

"Sorry?" Ellen spat the words at him. "What does something like you know about sorrow?" She turned to her brother as Ushig moved away. "Can I look at your arms, Davie?"

Obediently, her brother sat up and rolled up his sleeves. Together they studied the twin tracks of the trow's claws, just above each elbow. Davie had been lucky. On one arm, the trow hadn't broken the skin, and the scratches on the other didn't look too deep, though Ellen frowned when she saw how the blood welled up and trickled down his arm.

Davie looked into her face. "What's a *Teind,* Ellen? And what does he mean about the Wild Hunt? And another thing ..." He glanced up at the endless grey sky. "How can this place have a Queen of the Night? It never gets dark."

Ellen had struggled so hard to make Davie listen to her, but now at last the moment had arrived, and she realized she wasn't ready for it after all. She didn't want to tell him the things she knew, or suspected. "I'm not sure," she said at last. "There're lots of things here that aren't in the book."

Davie rubbed a hand across the scratches on his arm. "Well, there's nothing we can do about it just now. Let's just rest while we can."

They sat together for a while in silence, then Davie said, "That old woman — you said she was there to warn us of danger?"

Ellen nodded. Her eyes brimmed with tears. "I'm so sorry, Davie. I thought I was doing the right thing, but I couldn't remember it properly, and now ..."

"You would never have gone down there if she hadn't appeared." He laughed softly. "It's a bit ..."

"Chicken and egg?" suggested Ellen, grateful that he seemed to be feeling so much better.

They smiled at each other for a moment, then Ellen was horrified to see two fat tears squeeze out of Davie's eyes and roll down his face.

"Davie! Don't worry. We'll get away somehow."

"It's not that. Well, it is, partly." He reached up a grubby hand to wipe the tears away. "I've been such a fool! I let Ushig dazzle me with a bunch of stupid tricks."

"No, Davie," said Ellen. "It was a glamour — a spell."

Davie shook his head. "You're only here because you wanted to help me. And now I'm trapped." He swallowed. "I can't leave Ushig. I have to go with him. I suppose I deserve whatever's coming to me. But not you." He took a deep breath. "You'd be safe at home if it wasn't for me."

"Oh, Davie." Ellen felt tears rising in her own eyes. "It's not your fault. It's mine! I said the rhyme that brought Ushig."

"Well," said Davie, "I suppose we both made mistakes, but that doesn't matter. I want you to go back, Ellen. Ushig said you would be safe on the path. The seal folk will take care of you."

Ellen thought of the Sluach, dancing in the dust, and the woman shape that had led to that terrifying encounter with the trows. The path might be better than the forest itself, but it still wasn't safe, no matter what Davie thought.

She shook her head. "I'm staying with you," she said firmly. "Just try and stop me." They both knew Davie was in no state to do anything about it.

"I'm so sorry, Ellen."

"We're both sorry then," she said with false cheerfulness, forcing the words past the lump in her throat, "but at least I've got the real Davie back again."

Davie nodded, accepting her words. She would

not tell him again that it was her fault. But she knew it was — and she knew that when the moment came, she would have to pay whatever price was necessary to undo her mistake.

"Why are you sorry?" Ushig had walked down the path to join them.

"Ellen's my sister," said Davie. "And I've let her down." His face darkened and Ellen reached out to touch his hand.

"You have told me such things before." Ushig frowned. "You do not explain them properly."

At any other time, Ellen might have smiled to hear Ushig repeat more or less the same thing she had said to him. They truly did come from different worlds — though she was beginning to understand that the alien nature of their surroundings was not quite as important as the difference inside their heads.

She thought of her grandmother and the pain in her face when she spoke of Laura, the daughter she had lost. Clearly, some of the Peerie Folk could feel love. Maybe she should make one more effort to get Ushig to understand. If he did, he might change his mind and let them go. It was a faint hope, but she could think of nothing else that might help.

"We were born into the same family," she said. "We have the same mother and father. We've grown up together. We're ..." she struggled to find the right words. "We care about each other."

"Ah," said Ushig, "you are members of the same household. It is a question of honour. There is an obligation between you."

Ellen gave up. "No," she said wearily. "It's not an obligation. He's my brother and I love him. That's all."

The frown was back on Ushig's face.

"We'll just have to make the best of it," she said to Davie. "Together."

Davie made an effort. "Together," he agreed, with a watery smile.

Chapter 19

For the first time, Ellen witnessed Ushig's transformation with nothing to distract her. In mingled horror and fascination she watched the boy shape grow taller and wider, the hair on his head flowing swiftly down his back to form a dense black coat that soon covered the whole of his body.

She saw his limbs twist, heard bones creak and bend as he shifted from one shape to another, arms becoming legs, feet turning into hooves. His human face grew long and narrow and she heard him sigh as he stretched and shook himself, the black mane flying out from his head, like someone fitting themselves more comfortably into a new set of clothes.

The black horse nodded. Ellen resisted the urge to reach out and stop Davie as he stumbled towards it. Ushig bent one knee, lowering his body almost to the ground.

"Come on, Ellen." Davie scrambled on to his back and held out a hand. Seeing her hesitation, he added, "What have we got to lose?"

He was right. Her legs trembled as she walked over to join them, partly through fear and partly because she was so weak and shaky. She couldn't even manage to climb on to the back of the huge dark animal by herself.

Eventually, Davie reached out with his uninjured arm to haul her up. This time, the coarse black mane had not formed handcuffs round his wrist. She ended in an undignified sprawl, her head on one side and legs on the other. Ushig's tail snapped to and fro and his muscles bunched, as though she was some disrespectful fly he would sweep away if he could. Making an enormous effort, Ellen scraped her way to an upright position and wrapped her arms around her brother. With one final twitch of Ushig's tail, they set off.

For a long while, the path continued its endless meander among the trees, but there came a time when Ellen found she was gripping Davie more tightly, leaning into his back as the road grew steeper. It twisted first one way, then another, always moving higher. The trees crowding in on either side began to thin. Rocky outcrops reared up out of the greenery. White ribbons of water flowed down sheer walls of naked stone. Spaces opened up among the trees, the ground carpeted in huge piles of dead leaves, as though nothing had disturbed them since the world began.

Ushig plodded on, never looking up from the green road at his feet. The double burden he carried was a heavy one, even for him, but he never suggested they stop to rest or faltered in his determined progress towards the higher ground.

It was no longer moss underfoot. Now the road wove its way between huge boulders, Ushig's hooves slipped on rough grass and scrabbled over patches of grainy pebbles as the path grew steeper

still. Ellen clung tightly to Davie, who leaned
forward almost over Ushig's head to avoid sliding
off his back.

They emerged from between the rocks to find
themselves at the top of the hill. Ellen slid
gratefully to the ground and Davie followed. Ushig
hung his head, blowing great bellows of air in and
out of his lungs.

Ellen looked across at Davie and felt a surge of
fear at the sight of the blood still oozing through
his sleeve. Those scratches should have stopped
bleeding by now. The trow's claws hadn't done
much more than break the surface of the skin. The
one on her own hand had stopped long ago. And
it wasn't just the blood. Davie's eyes were cloudy
and his skin pale, as though his life's energy was
draining out of him with every drip of blood. A line
from the book came back to her in a sudden rush
of memory. *"A wound from a trow will never heal."*

"This really is Traprain Law," Davie said.
"Remember we came here once?"

Ellen nodded, though it wasn't exactly the same
as she remembered. In their own world, huge
stones littered the hilltop, but they were sunk deep
in the earth and far fewer than the double row of
standing stones, topped with massive slabs of rock,
that she saw here. The stones formed a covered
walkway round a circular patch of open ground.
She walked into the circle, vaguely hoping that it
represented some kind of safety.

She turned back to Davie. "Didn't Aunt Marian
say they found treasure here? That there used to
be a massive hill fort?"

"The Votadini lived here." Ushig was once more in human form. "Great warriors."

Ellen looked at the stone circle. If this had ever existed in her world, it had fallen into ruin long ago. She glanced back at Ushig. It was impossible to imagine what it must be like to live as long as he had.

Davie pointed to a bulky mass rising out of the distant sea. "Look! That's the Bass Rock."

He slumped back to the ground with a sigh, but Ellen stayed on her feet, turning in a slow circle, her gaze travelling from the vast flat expanse of the tideless sea, then inland, across the forest that clothed the world. It stretched out before her as far as she could see. And in this place, she could see a very long way. Her hand strayed to the glasses in her pocket. For some reason, they brought a vivid reminder of her mother and father.

Swallowing the sob that that rose in her throat, she pointed towards the shadowy shapes of distant mountains. "What's over there?"

Ushig frowned. "Whatever the Queen wills."

Yet again, an answer that was not really an answer. Ellen turned again, to see another huge rock looming out of the vast expanse of green. With a jolt of recognition, she realized she was looking at the rock that formed the heart of the city of Edinburgh, but there were no houses or streets. Instead, a shining lake encircled the great castle on the hill.

"Is that where the Queen lives?"

Ushig nodded.

"Then why did we come here?"

He looked at the castle, then back to Ellen.
"This is the place of the Wild Hunt," he said. The
Queen will come to us."

"Robert Kirk didn't say much about the Wild
Hunt," said Ellen, hoping that Ushig might give
her some useful information.

"Who is Robert Kirk?"

"The man who wrote my book!" Ellen answered
in surprise.

Ushig blinked, equally surprised. "So the Queen
did not, after all, call him by his true name." A
humourless smile appeared on his face. "Even so,
he would not want to remember the hunt."

Ellen turned away. She knew by now that if
Ushig didn't explain something, it was because he
didn't want to.

The sea was so still it looked almost solid,
as though you could walk on its glassy surface
without sinking. The seal folk were there. Her
grandmother. Her family. Desire tugged at her
heart as she sat down beside Davie, but it was
pointless to wish that she and her brother were
with them now.

She shifted uneasily as Ushig crouched down
beside her. He held out a handful of shells. She
looked at them blankly.

"Will you let me tell your fortune?" he asked.

Ellen shrugged in half-hearted agreement. At
least it might take her mind off things for a
moment or two.

With a sharp motion of his wrist, the wraith
tossed the shells on to a flat stone. Ellen looked
down as they scattered across the rough red

surface. All but one had rolled to the edge, leaving a single pink shell alone in the centre.

Ushig reached out and touched it with his finger. Then he looked into her eyes. "Trust your heart," he said. "It has served you well this far." Ignoring all the others, he tapped one solitary black and white shell that teetered on the edge of the stone, but did not fall. "This is one you think you know, but you do not." His voice was soft. "You do not know me, Ellen."

She frowned at him. It was the first time he had used her name. Then she stood up, rubbing her eyes. The last time she looked, the Bass Rock was clearly outlined against the sky. Now it was hard to make out the shape. All around her, the light was fading

"Davie," she said. "It's getting dark." There was no reply. She looked down at her brother. He sat with his back against the rock, his eyes closed.

A mournful howl echoed across the land and she turned quickly, sure she had glimpsed a dark shape slip from the shelter of one rock to another. From somewhere nearby she heard the faint jingle of harness bells.

"What's happening?"

"Night comes," said Ushig.

"But you said there was no night or day here. Didn't he, Davie?" She bent down and shook her brother, horrified to see how he lay slumped on the ground, his face a pale blur in the darkness. He opened his eyes and smiled at her. She heard the howl again, then another and another until the air was full of sound. The hairs on the back of her neck stood up and she spun round, peering into the gloom, trying to identify the source of the noise that seemed to come from all sides at once.

There was a stillness in the air, like the moment of calm before a storm. She turned back to Ushig. "What's going on?"

"It is the Queen," he said. "The world turns at her command."

Chapter 20

Ellen clenched her fists and shifted restlessly from foot to foot. The sense of urgency that filled her made it impossible to stand still and wait, but she had nowhere else to go.

"Ushig?" Her voice shook. "Won't you at least tell us why we're here?"

His answer, when it came, sent shivers down her back.

"You are here because the Wild Hunt must run and the Queen chose me to be its prey."

Ellen swallowed. Her throat was dry. "Is that what 'Teind' means?" Ushig nodded briefly in response. "But that doesn't explain why you brought us with you."

Davie pulled himself into a sitting position, cradling his injured arm on his lap. The bleeding still hadn't stopped.

"Did you come to our world to hide?" Davie's voice held a note of sympathy. "Why did you choose us? I don't think we've been much help."

"Ushig is not my true name." He spared a glance for Ellen. "I think your sister knows that." His eyes drifted back to Davie. "The Queen has my name. She draws me, as I draw you — but she gave me a choice. The Teind always has a choice."

"What choice?" Ellen asked, hoping against hope that the answer was not what she expected it to be.

Ushig's cold, inhuman eyes never left her brother's face. "If I can find another to take my place, then I become the hunter instead of the hunted."

Suddenly Ellen was no longer afraid. She was furious. "So that's why you didn't kill Davie when you had the chance! You're going to trade his life for your own!"

"I am a wraith," said Ushig. "I cannot die — although your brother can."

Ellen's fists clenched. "How can you do this?"

"We do as we are made to do." The wraith's odd-coloured eyes were hard. "All those who ride with the hunt have paid with the life of another."

"But you just said you can't die!" Ellen's voice shook with rage. She stepped in front of Ushig, shielding her brother from that predatory gaze.

Ushig looked down at her. "In this world, only the selkie have children. We others do not breed, for we do not grow old. But death has many forms. There are those who ride and there are those who carry them." He spat out the words as though they tasted bitter in his mouth, "I will not be caught and locked into a single shape. For me, it is worse than death."

"Davie never said he would take your place," shouted Ellen fiercely.

"Your brother's life is forfeit to me. Three times he has climbed on my back," answered Ushig. "It is his life I offer to the Queen, for it is mine to take." He pointed down the hill at the path they had followed. "The hunt is waking."

Faint lights, like will o' the wisp, danced up the road they had climbed a short time before. Ellen looked at them for a moment, then she knelt beside Davie. "Don't worry," she said. "Everything will be all right." Davie didn't answer.

"Ushig," she called softly, afraid that she might attract the notice of anything that lurked nearby, "Ushig, you have to help us."

The reply, when it came, was a whisper in her ear. "I will not give my life for your brother."

The rage burning inside her faded away, leaving nothing but dreary understanding. Ushig would not help them. It was impossible for him to feel guilt, friendship or even remorse.

The jingling was louder now. Blue sparks floated in the air, flashes of light erupting from the darkness, escorting a trail of horses winding their way uphill. The riders on their backs were enormously tall and thin, with pale faces showing no shadow of expression. As they entered the circle Ellen knew that Davie finally had his wish. They were face to face with the lords of this strange world.

In and out among the horses leaped hairy boggarts with leering faces and claws where their hands should be. Above them the air shivered with beating wings. Ellen stared up, mesmerized by the host of tiny creatures, some glittering like fireflies, others with twisted bodies and dark sooty wings.

The riders parted and a woman on a huge white horse moved towards them. Her long red hair was caught back from her forehead with a silver circle and fell from her shoulders to mingle with the billowing mass of her rich green cloak. Ellen caught her breath. She had never seen anyone so beautiful in her entire life.

Silver eyes glittered as the queen looked at the crowd gathered around her. She opened her mouth and everything went still. Her voice rang out across the hilltop. *"Form or shade, born or made, be welcome here."*

The host answered with a swelling cacophony of shrieks and laugher. She raised a hand and the noise stopped with a suddenness that made Ellen blink.

"Where is my Teind?" demanded the Queen. "Let him step forward."

Ellen still couldn't take her eyes off that perfect face. She felt Ushig move from her side.

"I see you, Ifrinn," he said.

Her outline shimmered in the moonlight. She was a woman still, but no longer red and green. Instead, an inky black cloud of hair lay across the folds of a pure white cloak. Her silver eyes studied Ellen for a long moment before she turned her attention back to the wraith.

"I see you, Ushig. You have come as you were bid. Or have you brought another to join our sport?"

"I have, my lady," said Ushig, his voice low. He gestured with one hand and Davie stumbled forward. The Queen tilted her head to look at him and Ellen glimpsed something inside the woman's shape, a tall column of light, so dazzling she was forced to shut her eyes. Even behind her closed lids, strands of colour wove in and out of each other, like the ribbon bridle she had used to trap Ushig. She blinked hard and opened her eyes. Ifrinn was a woman again.

"A human child," Ifrinn said thoughtfully. "There has not been a human child in this world for a long time." She flashed a look of approval at Ushig.

"There are two, my lady," said Ushig. "Daniel and Rose."

Ellen glanced at him in surprise. Hadn't Ushig told her he could not lie? It wasn't exactly a lie, though. He hadn't said those names belonged to the children he brought with him. But Ellen had no time to wonder why he chose to keep their true names from the Queen. Ifrinn was looking at her once more. It was only her shock at Ushig's unexpected behaviour that made it possible to fight the hypnotic power of that bright gaze.

The Queen smiled. "You have done well, Ushig," she said. "We will have even more sport with two."

"No!" Ushig took a step towards her. "The promise was for one."

The riders shifted and murmured, clearly taken aback by his words. Ellen stared at them and the coal black horses they rode. Was she mistaken or did the eyes of these horses burn with tormented madness. Perhaps they were wraiths, like Ushig. If so, then they must be those who had failed to escape the Wild Hunt — condemned to spend eternity locked into a single shape.

Ifrinn lifted her head and laughed. Music rang out across the darkening world. Ushig looked up at her, then lowered his head to stare at the ground as the Queen crooked her finger. Davie stumbled forward. Ellen tried to stop him, but somehow her hands could not catch hold. She felt her own feet lift, her legs taking her forward one step at a time behind Davie, both of them moving stiffly towards the woman who looked down at them, her lips turned upwards in a smile.

The Queen leaned forward. Placing her finger beneath Davie's chin, she lifted his head. Davie blinked, but he didn't flinch as Ifrinn stretched out with her other hand and touched the dark patch on his sleeve. She raised her finger to her lips. "His life blood tastes rich," she said to her companions.

"No! You can't have him!" Instead of pulling back against the force that drew her, Ellen dashed forward. She wrenched her brother away. Davie lurched to one side like a limp, life-size doll.

Reaching inside her top, she grabbed hold of the stone and pulled it from the string, holding it in her upraised fist.

"Ah," whispered the Queen, her eyes shining. "You have a weapon, do you think?" She lifted her hand once more

This time a silver swirl of light leaped from one delicate finger, spiralling across the darkness and through the hole in the middle of the charm. Ellen gasped in pain as the light brushed her skin. Blisters were already forming on her wrist as the light drew back towards the Queen, carrying the charm along with it.

Ifrinn tilted her head and looked down at it with

mild curiosity, then she snapped her wrist. Her fingers closed around the stone. When she opened them again, there was nothing in her hand but a pile of withered leaves. Her eyes glittered like shards of ice.

"It seems your protection has failed you." She leaned over towards Davie, her mouth open in a feral smile. "Run you will, my lad. One way or another, you will run." Then she turned to Ellen. "What do you say, little one? Will you leave him to me?"

Ellen stiffened. She knew it was her fault they were here. All her fault. Davie was weakened by the injury on his arm and that, too, was thanks to her. This was the moment she had feared ever since Ushig told her why they were here. It took all her strength to force herself forward.

"Take me," she said, her voice little more than a whisper, "and let my brother go."

There was a long silence. The fear Ellen felt struck to the very depths of her being, drowning out the little voice inside that told her this was all her fault and she was the one who should pay the price. But the words were out now. There was no way she could take them back. As the silence continued, she began to hope that, at least, it was not too late for Davie.

Ifrinn looked around at the horsemen. "Will she do?"

"Aye, take her," they shouted.

A glint of amusement appeared in the Queen's eyes. "We shall take both. Let us see how long she runs beside her brother."

A seed of anger took root in Ellen's heart when she realized that her sacrifice was all for nothing. She opened her mouth to protest, even though she knew it was useless, but Ushig got there first.

"That is unjust! One for one was the promise! Not two!"

The Queen ignored him. "A storm!" she declared. "We shall have a storm!" All eyes turned to the sky. Ifrinn raised her hand and Ellen saw Ushig lift his face along with the rest. The pearly grey twilight was darkening towards night. Light bled from the sky, falling straight towards Ifrinn's outstretched hand. The moon appeared, slipping in and out of the clouds as she tilted her palm upwards to catch the raindrops that began to fall, slowly at first, then faster and faster.

She looked at Ellen and Davie. "This is my gift to you. Ford the river and reach the stone gateway upon the hill, then you will be free."

"What river? What stone?" Ellen's anger gave her courage. This was no gift — only a tantalizing promise that would never be kept.

Ifrinn smiled in what looked almost like approval. "Follow the water," she said. "Find your way through the forest and you will have a chance to win your freedom."

She pointed at Ushig. "Your game is over," she said. "Now you join the hunt, as I promised you should. Man or beast, it is your choice."

Once again Ellen saw Ushig blur and reform, into a coal black horse with wild red eyes. Ifrinn's hand fell. "You have until midnight," she told the children, then she turned her horse.

Harness bells jingled as the riders spun round to follow her. A rush of wind buffeted Ellen and Davie so that they staggered where they stood. Horses and riders poured down the hill, splitting and reforming as they galloped past the huge slabs of rock that stood like sentinels on the bare hilltop.

A single, riderless horse melted into the host. Ellen watched them sweep down the hillside until they disappeared, taking Ushig along with them. Hoofbeats faded into the distance, leaving the children alone on the rain-soaked hillside.

Chapter 21

Davie tilted his head and looked up at the moon. He blinked hard, rubbed his eyes and said, "Where's Ushig?"

"He's gone," said Ellen. "The Queen took him."

From the corner of her eye she glimpsed something small and dark. It let loose a snigger and scuttled between the rocks. The boggarts and some of those other, nameless things must have stayed behind. Maybe they liked to follow the prey instead of the hunters. Or maybe they were there to drive them in one particular direction.

A breeze tickled her cheek, driving the rain into her face. She shivered. The air was much colder now.

Davie frowned and put a hand up to his forehead. "The Queen ... she said we had to run ..."

"Don't you remember?"

The frown deepened. "There were blue lights ... and horsemen ... other things too." He shook his head. "It's all a bit hazy."

Ellen was glad to see that her brother was no longer the helpless doll that Ifrinn had treated with such casual contempt, but her relief was short-lived. A long, drawn out howl in the distance reminded her of the need to hurry.

"It doesn't matter," she said urgently. "We have to get out of here, Davie. The Wild Hunt is coming. We have to find the river. We have to go back, into the forest."

The Queen's gifts were tainted. "She gives you hope, but always there is poison at its heart." Those were Ushig's words, after they escaped from the trows. She now realized how right he was. But it was the only hope they had.

Davie shook the raindrops from his hair and looked into his sister's frightened eyes. "They're coming for both of us, aren't they?"

Ellen nodded. "We have until midnight. Then the hunt begins."

"We'd better go then," said Davie, his voice grim. He walked out of the stone circle and a little way down the hill, Ellen following behind him, but then he stopped.

"Come on, Davie." She tugged his sleeve, careful to avoid his injury. "Please. We have to go."

"Wait, let me think a minute." He looked at her. "Water flows downhill. If we can find a stream and follow the water, then eventually it's got to flow into the river."

That must have been what the Queen meant, thought Ellen, though in this strange world, things might be different from their own. She said nothing. There was no point.

Another howl rang across the night. The noise was closer this time. A flash of lightning lit the sky behind them. Ellen looked back and her heart jumped. A massive shape stood in the centre of the circle, silhouetted against the sky. A crown of antlers sprang from his head, and his huge body was covered from head to foot in a heavy cloak of animal skins.

It took her a moment to realize that the things twisting and turning at his feet were dogs. They were not like any she had ever seen before. Narrow, snake-like bodies undulated around the monstrous hunter, their eyes pinpricks of flame in the gloom. From time to time they lunged forward with sudden sharp movements, as though desperate to follow their prey. The only thing that kept them in check was the handful of ropes the hunter held in his fist.

Thunder shook the world around them. Davie, too, turned to look and gasped in shock. "When is it midnight?" His voice was a whisper.

"I don't know." Ellen grabbed her brother's shoulder and spun him round. "Let's get out of here."

Their feet slipping on wet grass and loose stones, stumbling over knotty roots, they set off once again, moving as fast as they dared over the rough ground. At the bottom of the slope, they paused to listen.

"This way," said Ellen, heading for the faint gurgle of water. She forced her way through a tangle of bushes to find a little trickle running downhill towards the forest. Davie hurried behind her. Neither of them mentioned the rustling leaves and faint giggles that told them there were other things nearby, following their progress with obvious interest.

Their invisible attendants did nothing to interfere with them and there was no indication of pursuit. Not yet. Soon the little rill of water joined up with another, and another, till they were hurrying along beside a stream. Ellen began to hope that Davie was right. Eagerly she looked around, but there was no sign of a hill, or the stone that held their one hope of escape.

Once they entered the forest, she had no time to think of anything except the struggle to move forward. The wide-branched trees gave them protection from the wind and rain, but this was not the green road, where the tangled wildwood stepped aside to leave a clear and easy path. They slowed down almost to a crawl as they clambered over fallen tree trunks and staggered over heaps of smooth rock washed up along the banks of the tumbling stream, their heads bent at an awkward angle to avoid the branches that hung down almost to the ground.

Once they almost lost the stream altogether, when it reached a huge slab of rock, flowing down in a series of tumbling waterfalls that left them no alternative except to fight their way up the bank and into the trees before they could swing back to find the water again. Sometimes the only way forward was to take to the stream and they waded knee-deep through the icy water, past places where the bank was too steep or the trees too close to allow them to walk alongside.

Davie soon lost patience with the branches that grabbed at the torn sleeves of his sweatshirt. Eventually he pulled it off and dumped it. Ellen said nothing. The wind was colder now and both of them were soaked, but they were red-faced and sweating from the effort of struggling through a forest alive with a hostile determination to slow them down.

But all the time the stream grew wider, until at last the opposite bank was no more than a dim shadow in the moonlight.

"Do you think this is the river?" Ellen asked as they paused to catch their breath after a particularly rocky scramble.

Before Davie had a chance to answer, the distant blare of a horn and the excited yapping of a pack of dogs told them that somewhere in the darkness behind them, the hunt had finally begun.

They heard a snigger in the bushes. Ellen turned her head, but there was nothing to see. She hurried on, Davie close behind her. It was getting harder and harder for him to keep up. When she turned back to mutter words of encouragement, she saw that his wounded arm still oozed blood. It sapped his strength so much that for once it was Ellen's shorter legs that set the pace.

The river, when they finally reached it, was unmistakable ... and impossible. It was obvious that the Queen had been enjoying a joke at their expense. No human body could survive that boiling mass of foam, the thundering force of water that endlessly split and reformed, constantly reshaped by the rocks beneath its surface

Ellen stared across the unbridgeable gap at their one hope of freedom, a hill crowned by two huge standing stones, with another laid on top to form a doorway. The stones that glittered enticingly in the moonlight might as well have been on the moon. Even if she had been fit and well rested instead of filthy and exhausted, her face and hands stinging from innumerable scrapes and scratches, there was no chance she could ever swim through that turbulent expanse of water to reach the other bank.

Davie sank to his knees. "It's over," he said. "We're finished."

Chapter 22

Ellen looked down at Davie and then at the tumbling water.

She knew she should be afraid — she should be terrified, with the hunt on her heels and that turbulent barrier between her and their only hope of escape. A burst of noise from among the trees triggered a shiver of dread that rocked her from head to foot. But the sight of the water soothed her fear. It called to her with such strength that it took a conscious effort not to move forward. It drew her, like Ushig had drawn Davie.

The thought was like a slap in the face. Sweat ran down her face. She began to itch all over. She gasped in shock as she raised a hand to wipe her forehead and saw the flaps of skin that joined one finger to the next.

Her fingers brushed her hair. It felt different, shorter and denser than she was used to. And the hairs on her upraised arm were changing, growing thick and dark, like a coat of fur. Her fingers explored her face. It too, was changing shape.

Her rising panic dissolved as a spark of understanding pierced her confusion and she let out a gasp of wonder and delight. She was no longer human. She was not a selkie either, but something different ... something in between.

"Davie," she breathed, hardly daring to believe it was true. "Look!"

Her brother glanced up and jumped to his feet, weariness forgotten. Ellen registered the horror on his face and a picture of what she must look like flashed into her mind. A half-human, half animal face, a body covered in fur. No longer Ellen, but a creature out of nightmare.

"What are you?" He grabbed her by the shoulders, his fingers digging savagely into her skin. "What have you done with my sister?"

She recoiled from the pain and anger in his eyes. "No, Davie! It's me. It's Ellen!" Her eyes filled with tears as he glared at the alien creature his sister had become.

"It's the selkie blood, Davie — this world brings out the selkie blood! Can't you feel it?" She pleaded with him, her voice hoarse with urgency. "Don't you see? We can change — we can cross the water!"

At last she saw understanding blossom. "It's Ellen," he muttered, more to himself than to her. "It's still Ellen." He dropped his hands from her shoulders and stared down at them, frowning even harder. Then he shook his head. "It's no good. I can't feel anything."

Ellen kicked off her shoes and pulled at Davie's arm, tugging him towards the water. "You can feel it if you try, I know you can," she pleaded. "Look at the river. Can't you feel it calling you?" She stared into his face, hoping desperately that the changes in her own body would be reflected in his. "Try, Davie. Please try."

He turned his head to look at the water, then closed his eyes. "I'm sorry," he said at last. "I can't do it."

"Davie, you must!"

They both jumped as a howl sounded from the woods.

"They're coming," Davie said. "They're coming for me, but not for you. This is your chance, Ellen. You have to get away."

"No." She looked into his eyes. "I won't leave you."

"Please," begged Davie. "Mum and Dad need one of us to come back."

Ellen glanced at the tumbling water, then back at Davie, standing pale-faced and trembling beside her. There was only one answer.

"No Davie. You're wrong. They wouldn't want me to leave you." Numb with despair, she reached out and took his hand.

They stood together with their backs to the forest, staring with hopeless longing at the shining gate across the river while the wild hunt drew closer. Soon, now, it would be over.

Ellen heard the crash of animal bodies as they forced their way through the bushes behind her. Then something broke the surface of the water. She should have guessed the Queen would take no chances. Even if they had managed to make it this far, she had sent her servants ahead to stop them getting any further. Their exhausting flight through the forest had been for nothing.

She caught her breath as another dark head bobbed into view, and another, until the river was a tumbling mass of sleek furry bodies.

"Hurry!" Skarra's voice called out from among the crowd that thronged the water's edge. "The hunt is almost here!"

"Davie," she whispered, hardly daring to believe it. "It's the seal folk!"

Without hesitation, Ellen clenched her hand tightly round her brother's, dragging him along with her in a wild leap out over the water and beneath the surface. Her momentary panic dissolved when she felt her webbed fingers and toes driving easily through the water.

Her clothes dragged at her, but warm furry bodies closed in all around, eager to help. She let Davie go, knowing he was safe with their seal folk cousins. Something — someone, she corrected herself — nudged sharply at her arms and she opened them wide to embrace warm, living flesh.

She had no need to draw breath. Her lungs were still filled with air. The water around her felt almost like a living thing, strong in places, weak in others. Despite her sodden clothes, her body moved more smoothly through the water than it ever could before, twisting and turning through the churning tumult towards the opposite shore.

They were only just in time. Behind them the snake-like dogs exploded from between the trees. She glanced back to see a horde of red-eyed snarling beasts, animals twice the size of any normal dog, their skinny muscular bodies straining forward before they turned and snapped at each other for want of better prey.

A huge figure emerged from the darkness. From this distance, Ellen should have been able to see nothing but shadows. And it was true; some of that towering shape *was* impossible to make sense of. Were those human legs? Or animal? Was it a cloak that covered his body, or a heavy coat of fur? But when Ellen looked into the face beneath the towering crest of antlers, the distance between them faded away and she found herself transfixed. Yellow eyes with vertical black pupils stared into her own, confident and calculating, filled with an intense hunger that she knew would only be satisfied when he finally came face to face with his prey.

The hunter stood at the water's edge, looking down at the river, then he raised a horn and blasted out a call that echoed into the dark sky above them. An answering call split the night and Ellen saw a line of horses step out along the bank, all of them black, save one.

A horse so white it shimmered in the moonlight picked its way down the slope, the rider on its back no longer a woman, but a coiling mass of red, green and silver light, intense enough to blind any living thing that looked too close or too long.

The seal folk sped across the water, sleek heads bobbing all around, each one leaving an arrow-shaped wake as they headed for the opposite shore. From behind came the slap of bodies hitting the water, accompanied by yelps of pain. The selkie were doing their best to keep the hounds from catching up. As her exhaustion began to recede a little, Ellen risked another glance behind and gasped in horror at the sight of the dog pack skimming across the surface towards her while seal folk reached up to pull them down. The water boiled with the violence of the struggle, but it wasn't going to be enough. There were too many of the red-eyed beasts and not enough selkie.

She turned back to the shore and saw with surprise that they were almost there. Ahead of her, only a short distance away, was the grassy mound, the white stone doorway shimmering at its summit, framing a blackness deeper than any she had ever seen. Within that blackness, she knew, was their promise of safety.

"Davie," she called out. "It's the gate!"

The comforting bodies on either side turned away and she staggered forwards out of the water. Davie appeared a moment later and together they stumbled up the rocky bank, running desperately for the gate that loomed above them, a message of hope that was almost too much to bear.

"Hurry, Ellen. Hurry." Her brother forced the words from his throat with barely the breath to move, let alone speak.

Ellen turned to look at him and gasped in horror. Davie had fallen once more.

He cradled his wounded arms and looked up at her with desperate urgency. "Go. Just go."

Some of the hounds had already reached the shore and were loping towards them, long red tongues dangling from their jaws.

"No Davie. I won't go without you," she said, though her voice quavered with fear.

She grabbed him by the arms and dragged him up the slope, fighting her way across thorny bushes and over patches of rough stone that tore the skin of her bare feet until they bled. She tripped over a heather root and fell heavily to the ground, the impact knocking the breath from her body.

With tears in her eyes, she hauled at Davie's back. "Get up, Davie! Get up! Please — just a little bit further!"

Sobbing now, Ellen stared up at the black heart in the centre of the white stone doorway, so close ... and yet an impossible distance away.

And then a dark shadow broke from the trees that clothed the land around the bare hilltop. A black horse with burning eyes galloped towards them, brushing against the nearest hound, sending it spinning with a flash of its razor hooves.

But there were so many others. The horse thudded to a halt as the snake dogs circled, snapping forward with mouths agape, leaping back to be replaced by another, and another. Ellen knew they had only seconds left before one of them would find its target and open the way for all the rest.

"Come up!" Ushig's voice called out, reverberating through the night. Ellen stared at the huge black horse with its mad eyes. This had started with Ushig and she saw now that it would end with him too.

There was nothing left but the utterly illogical belief that, despite everything, Ushig wished them no harm. With a strength born of sheer terror, she took hold of Davie, forcing him to his feet. She leaped on to Ushig's back and reached down to drag her brother up and over the body of the horse as though he were nothing more than a sack of potatoes.

A howl of rage set the whole night trembling. A hound jumped towards them, raking its claws across Ushig's flank as the horse galloped uphill towards the stones. Despite her terror, Ellen felt a sudden sharp sense of loss for a world she would never see again and then, with a leap that almost dislodged the two children clinging to his back, Ushig soared into the blackness and out the other side.

Chapter 23

Ellen found herself in total darkness, surrounded by water with no way of knowing what was up and what was down. Her body was human once more and she thrashed wildly, struggling to keep air in her lungs. Something nipped her back and she kicked out in panic. At last her head broke the surface. She gulped for air, coughing and spluttering as a salty wave slapped her face.

"Ellen, hold still!"

It was Ushig, his heavy horse body moving with a strange grace through the choppy water. She blinked to clear the stinging salt from her eyes and saw with relief that Davie still lay across his back.

Ushig grabbed her jacket in his teeth and she slung one arm round his neck, reaching out for Davie with the other, holding him steady as the horse pushed against the waves. Her feet scraped rough shingle and her panic evaporated. They were not lost in a wilderness of water after all.

Soon the waves were no higher than her knees. Davie slid from Ushig's back to land beside her. He groaned and opened his eyes, then coughed and spat.

"Come on, Davie," she said. With one last great effort, she put her arm around him. Leaning into each other, they staggered up the beach towards a deep cleft in the rock. Ellen collapsed backwards on to the shingle, her chest heaving, and stared up at the sky.

Above her, the stars were fading. A rose pink tinge spread across the sky. There was no dawn in the world ruled by the Queen of the Night. Hardly daring to believe it, she sat up and reached out an arm to brush the rough, barnacle encrusted rock.

"Davie," she whispered, tears of relief flooding her eyes. "It's Aldhammer — our Aldhammer! We made it!"

"Indeed we did." Ushig was a boy again. He sat in the shadows, watching as Davie sat up and looked at his sister.

"It was you, Ellen. You and Ushig brought me back."

"You look funny," she said. "You're covered in sand."

Davie smiled at her and Ellen smiled in return as she leaned back against the rock. Something was digging into her. She reached into her pocket and pulled out her glasses. They were a bit wonky and bent out of shape, but not broken. That was good. She would need them now. A deep sense of gladness filled her at the knowledge that she was really, truly home. Gently, she slipped them on, but quickly pulled them off again when she discovered the lenses were crusted in salt from her freezing cold swim. It didn't matter, though. Very soon now, she would be safe in Aunt Marian's house where she could take all the time she wanted to get them clean again.

She pushed her hair back from her forehead and

peered at Ushig. "Why didn't you tell me what you were going to do?"

Ushig shrugged. "I could not even tell myself. As long as we were on the Queen's business, we had the safety of the green road. And Ifrinn would never have opened that gate if she thought there was any chance you might reach it." He grinned. "Have I learned friendship, Ellen?"

She smiled at the dim figure half hidden among the rocks. "I think maybe you have."

Ushig's face grew thoughtful. "I like this world of yours, Ellen. There is much to interest me here. I promise you, I can be other than what I was made to be."

Ellen studied his face. There was a lightness in his eye that she had not seen before. Maybe it was true. Maybe a water wraith could learn to be human. "What changed your mind?"

"You did. When you refused to let me take Davie, I felt something within me. Something ... new. Then you refused to abandon him. When you offered yourself in his place, I understood a little of what you felt."

Someone laughed, almost in her ear. Ellen twisted round, her sodden clothes clinging to her body like an icy second skin. Had Aisil braved the land to welcome them home? She peered into the gloomy interior of the rock and felt her heart give one great thump. The figure in the shadows was not Aisil. It was Ifrinn. The Queen had come to the sea after all.

Ellen heard Ushig take a deep breath. Beside her, Davie pushed himself up till he stood with his back against the rocks. Slowly, she rose to join him.

"I see you, Ushig." Ifrinn stepped to the edge of the cleft, her pale body glimmering in the darkness. It seemed she had brought her own light along with her.

"I do not see you, Ifrinn." Ushig's voice was tense but determined. "This is not your place." He walked forward a little. "Are you not afraid, Lady, this close to the sea? Its creatures are not yours to command."

"How sad it must be for you, then, to know you have no more salt in your body than a freshwater trout." Ifrinn's voice was filled with scorn.

Ellen turned to look at Ushig and saw him raise his hand, sending a handful of shells flying across the space between him and the Queen. Droplets of sea water sparkled like jewels as they passed through a single beam of early morning sunshine lighting the nooks and crannies in the rock above their heads.

The shells scattered across the silver gown and Ellen felt a surge of hope as she saw the colours begin to spread, like paint in water, patches of pink and brown, black and red, bleeding into the silver. Ifrinn looked down, her eyebrows bent in a puzzled frown. Once more Ellen heard that tinkling laugh.

"Such paltry toys." Ifrinn brushed the shells away with a careless hand until her gown was once more pure silver. She turned her attention back to Ushig. "So you thought to escape through one of my own gates?"

"I could not do it for myself," said the water wraith. "You were kind enough to do it for me."

Ifrinn's eyes glittered. "Do not play games, Ushig. These two are mine. One was promised and the other one I chose." The silver eyes looked straight at Ellen. "One of the seal folk for my own," she murmured. "How very amusing!" Then she held out one long pale arm. "Come, Rose. Come, Daniel."

Ellen leaned back against the rocks for support. She felt Davie's elbow brush hers and knew that he was trembling too. Ifrinn's face was so very beautiful, the longing and welcome in her eyes so full of promise that Ellen almost took a step towards her. But she did not move and, without her true name, it seemed that the Queen of the Night could not completely blind her to the truth.

Ifrinn's perfect face creased in a puzzled frown and her hand fell to her side. The finger of sunlight crept across the rocks above her.

"The water is rising," said Ushig. "Will you let it trap you here?"

No one moved. There was no sound except the gentle fall of waves upon the shingle.

At last Ifrinn spoke. "If you will not come willingly," she said, "then I must take you."

Once more she raised her hand. Ellen gasped. Pain shot through her body, as though her blood was on fire. Fear blossomed as she realized her legs were no longer under her control. First with one foot, then the other, Ellen moved to where Ifrinn stood waiting.

Something nibbled at Ellen's mind, something important, if only she could hook it and reel it in. Ifrinn did not like the sea. But why? She had no fear of any other water. Voices tumbled around in Ellen's head. Ushig, telling her there was no light in the world except through Ifrinn's gift. Davie's voice from the day it all began, when she watched the sunlight dance across the surface of the pool. The queen hoarded light. What would happen if the light from another world met the light that was Ifrinn?

Ellen fought to ignore the pain that swept through her in dizzying waves. Her thoughts scrabbled frantically to and fro, seeking a way out like a rat in a maze. The sound of Davie's shuffling steps broke her concentration. She clenched her fists so that her glasses dug painfully into the palm of her hand.

Davie reached out and let his hand rest for a moment on his sister's arm. Then he stepped forward, blocking her from Ifrinn's grasping reach. "You can have me," he quavered, staring hard at Ifrinn, "but I'll never let you take my sister."

"Get down!" Fuelled by a surge of exasperation at her brave and foolish brother, Ellen pushed him away and lifted her other arm high in the air. It was only the slimmest of chances, but then, it had been that way from the beginning ... saying the rhyme; making the bridle; even the unexpected appearance of the seal folk to help them across the river. Ellen wasn't going to give up. She would *never* give up.

She caught the solitary sunbeam in the lens of her glasses and tilted her hand so that it shone straight into the darkness. A small spot of light winked into existence on the silver that was Ifrinn.

It was like an explosion on the surface of the sun. The light bounced, sending ripples of red, green, blue and violet spreading swiftly outwards. Ellen glimpsed pale eyes, wide with shock and surprise, then Ifrinn threw back her head and howled in rage and pain. The woman vanished. A column of light erupted into the air. The whole world trembled with the sound of Ifrinn's scream and Ellen clapped her hands over her ears as the noise burrowed relentlessly inside her head.

The towering shape grew brighter still, a dazzling shaft of pure white light that stretched out and up and then soared away into the dawn sky like a shooting star in reverse.

Faint in the distance, Ellen heard the tinkling of harness bells. Beside her, Davie gave a deep sigh and slid to the ground.

Chapter 24

Ellen flinched as a white shape swooped down from the sky. Then the mournful cry of a seagull broke the silence. She felt the soft touch of webbed fingers across her cheek and turned to see Aisil standing behind her.

"That was bravely done. And clever too."

Aisil reached out her other hand to Davie, who smiled up at her as she pulled him to his feet. With her arms wrapped around them both, Aisil turned her attention to the dark figure standing in the shadows.

Her head tilted as she studied Ushig. "I am in your debt," she said at last.

Ushig gave a small nod of acknowledgement and Aisil smiled. "You will always find a welcome with the seal folk." The smile widened. "Though I am not sure what the rest of this world will make of you."

The dark figure shifted slightly. "That is something we will no doubt find out."

Ellen smiled at the note of anticipation in his voice.

"Come on, Ellen," said Davie. He grinned at his sister. "It's time to go home."

Beyond the rocks, the houses of Aldhammer

crowded down towards the shore as they had always done. A plastic bag whipping across the coarse brown sand with the looming bulk of the power station in the distance brought a deep sense of satisfaction.

"I will see you again?" Aisil's hopeful voice broke into her thoughts. "I will come to the shore. It would be good to know my grandchildren a little better."

Ellen knew what that offer meant to Aisil, who had spent so many unwilling years in Aldhammer. Her steps slowed. She pictured the cove, the rocks and the water crowded with the seal folk and their children. A slow smile spread across her face. Perhaps that other world was not lost to her after all. She giggled. It was a bit like riding a bicycle. If you did it once, it was easy to do it again.

"I don't think you need to come here, to me," she said to Aisil.

Her grandmother's face crumpled and Ellen grabbed her hands. "No, that's not what I mean!" She turned to her brother. "Davie can't do it, can you, Davie?"

Davie shivered and shook his head. "No," he said, "and I don't want to."

Ellen laughed. She turned back to her grandmother. "You said the selkie blood was strong in me — and you were right! I'm not like you, but I'm not like other people either. I think, maybe, I can come to you."

Aisil smiled, but Davie looked anxious.

"What about the Queen?"

"You are right, Davie," said Aisil. "She is not so

easy to destroy — but it will be a long time before she recovers her strength," she added reassuringly.

Ellen was puzzled. Aisil did not seem surprised by her astounding news. Her expression when she looked at Ellen was one of delight.

"Not just my children then. It flows in my granddaughter too."

Ellen stared. "You mean Marian ...?"

Aisil shook her head. "Not Marian. Your selkie gift comes to you through your mother."

"Mum?" Davie's voice lifted in surprise. "Mum can do that? You're not serious!"

"Laura fears the sea for a reason she will not acknowledge," said Aisil. "She is afraid of a longing that she does not understand. But you ..." she turned to Ellen, "you understand that longing and you are not afraid."

Before Ellen had a chance to answer her, they heard a familiar voice ring out.

"Ellen! Davie!"

Ellen barely had time to absorb the sight of Marian running full tilt towards them before she was swept up in a hug so fierce she thought her bones might break. Marian held them both for a long moment, then she let go and looked at them, her eyes brimming with tears. She caught sight of Davie's arms and gasped in horror.

"Davie! What happened?"

"It's okay," said Davie. "See? They're not bleeding any more."

Marian began to rummage frantically in her pockets. For a moment, Ellen thought she was about to produce some sort of first aid kit. Instead, she pulled out a phone and handed it to Davie.

"I borrowed this. Call your mum and dad. They're absolutely frantic with worry. The police are searching the canal. They found Ellen's ribbons."

As Davie took the phone, Marian brushed Ellen's cheek with one finger. "At least I knew you had Davie to look out for you."

"No," said Davie, with a quiet glance at his sister. "It was Ellen who looked out for me."

Ellen watched him move up the slope in search of a better signal, then she looked back at Marian, taking in her tousled hair and rumpled clothes, the dark shadows under her eyes.

"How long have you been waiting?"

Marian looked blank. "I don't know. A long time ... it got dark."

"Only one night?" Ellen couldn't believe it. But then, in a world without night or day, how could you tell how much time had passed?

"What did you tell Laura?" Aisil's voice was soft, almost hungry as she spoke her other daughter's name.

Marian glanced at her mother, then back to Ellen. "I said I thought you might be coming back here, that I had an argument with you before you got on the train because you and Davie didn't want to leave Aldhammer. I didn't know *what* to say. I just ..." she stopped, her eyes fixed on a shape lurking in the shadows. She stepped in front of Ellen.

"What are you doing here?" Her voice had changed, no longer breathless, but hard and unforgiving. "You have made a great mistake if you think you can pursue them any further."

Ellen looked from her aunt to Ushig, who was watching their reunion with avid interest. "No." She tugged her aunt's arm, but Marian ignored her.

"Aunt Marian, listen to me," insisted Ellen. "You've got it wrong. It was Ushig who saved us. Without him, we would never have made it back." She looked at her grandmother for support.

Aisil nodded. "Ellen is right. The wraith fought against all that he is to bring them safely home again."

Ushig took a step forward into the morning sunlight. He bent down and scooped up a handful of broken shells from the place where Ifrinn had stood, and gazed at them thoughtfully for a moment before he opened his fist and let them fall. Then he looked up.

"I will leave now. I have a world to explore."

He glanced at Ellen, his eyes sparkling with anticipation, then he turned towards the rocks.

"Ushig, wait!"

Ellen had so much she wanted to say. That she understood now how hard he had struggled to turn away from the creature he once was, how brave he had been to challenge the power of the Queen and how grateful she was for his help ... but it was all jumbled together inside her head. In the end, all she could manage was a quiet, "Good luck."

He stared at her for a moment, then he bent forward. She felt his breath drift past her ear.

"My name is Dart."

He turned away and began to scramble up the
rocks, moving swiftly from one foothold to another.
He paused at the top and looked down at her.

"If you call me, Ellen, I will come."

"What did he say?" Marian asked, when Ellen
walked back to join her and Aisil.

"Nothing important." But Ellen knew Ushig
had offered a gift of friendship and trust that she
would treasure forever.

She frowned a little. A creature from another
world, set free to roam in this one? But then she
shook her head. He wasn't Ushig the water wraith.
Not any more. His name was Dart — and he was
her friend.

Author's Note

Ushig is an invented name from my own imagination. It has its roots in the Gaelic *"each uisge"* meaning "water horse".

Robert Kirk is real. He was minister of the Highland parish of Aberfoyle. One night he went out walking on Doon Hill and was stolen out of this world by the fairies.

His book, *The Secret Commonwealth of Elves, Fauns and Fairies,* describes an "Invisible World", inhabited by creatures that exist in parallel with our own.

Annemarie Allan

Hox

Twelve-year-old Robbie is angry and frustrated. Because of his father's work, he has to spend the weekend at the Institute for Animal Research.

A disturbing encounter changes everything. Suddenly, he is thrust into a perilous journey through the harsh landscape of a Highland winter, accompanied by two unexpected and mysterious travelling companions.

Read on for a taste of Robbie's adventure in Hox

Robbie crossed the grass and pressed the entry buzzer. After a few moments, he saw a bearded face at the tiny window, jaws busily working. Robbie had never seen Joe without a piece of gum in his mouth.

"Hi there, stranger!" Joe's voice held a strong hint of a mid-western drawl but Robbie had known him all his life. And knew that the closest Joe had ever been to cowboy country was a weekend trip to New York.

Joe stood and chewed, eyeing Robbie thoughtfully until he finally made up his mind. "Okay," he said. "You don't look very dangerous to me. Come on in."

"Hi." Robbie stepped gratefully inside, knowing Joe was bending, if not breaking, the rules. Only members of the research staff were allowed in the animal house. He smiled and reached up a hand to wipe his sweaty forehead, wondering why he felt so wobbly all of a sudden.

"Thought you were going away this weekend," said Joe, leading the way across the reception area towards an inner door.

"We were supposed to go to the cottage." Robbie made no effort to keep the resentment out of his voice. "But Dad said he had to work today."

"That's a pity." Joe slid a swipe card out of his shirt pocket and unlocked the door. "Don't think I'd fancy it myself, though. Must get pretty cold up there at this time of year."

"It does," said Robbie, just to be polite. He didn't care how cold it was. He loved going to the cottage. Last winter, they had arrived to find that the snow plough had only cleared the main roads. His dad had refused to risk the car on the potholed track up to the cottage and had tried to persuade Robbie that they might as well give up. But Robbie had eventually convinced him that they could walk the rest of the way and carry what they needed on their backs.

Robbie treasured the memory of the long trudge through the woods with nothing to break the stillness of the air except the creak of snow-laden branches, the crunch of their footsteps and the sound of their own laboured breathing. And most satisfying of all, that warm sense of coming home, when they finally emerged from the dim green tunnel to see the paint-blistered front door and the deep-set windows of the little house.

Joe tucked the swipe card into his shirt pocket. "I was sure your dad would sell that place when your grandmother died."

Joe was right. His father often talked about selling it. But he could do nothing until Robbie was old enough to agree. And Robbie knew he would never do that. He loved the place too much.

"He can't," said Robbie. "Grannie left it to me. It's *mine!*"

Joe chewed his gum a little harder and Robbie bit his lip, knowing he sounded like a spoiled brat. But his first sight of the huge room beyond the two locked doors drove the momentary embarrassment out of his head.

He had expected a bustling, crowded space filled with people. But the building was silent and empty. No one occupied the row of labs stretching all the way down one side of the building and, as far as he could see, there were no animals at all in the pens and cages that filled the open area in the middle.

"Where is everyone?" Robbie's voice sounded small and insignificant in the vast, echoing space.

"Get real, Robbie. You don't think I'd have let you in if there was anybody else around, do you?"

Robbie coughed. The stale, musty odour at the back of his throat was a strong reminder that this place had been home to a whole range of different creatures. He gestured at the empty cages. "But where are all the animals?"

Joe looked around, chewing fast again. "Used to be a lot busier than this," he agreed. "Especially when your mother was here. We made a good team, the three of us. But things got slower and slower after Jane died." He caught himself and looked down at Robbie with embarrassed sympathy. "Sorry."

"It's okay." Robbie knew all about his mother's trip to a conference in Bulgaria, when his unexpected early arrival had been followed by an infection the doctors could not control.

When he was younger, he used to believe he could remember a soft touch on his face, a whisper in his ear, even though he knew she died only a few days after he was born. Sometimes, he wished she was still here, but then at other times, he wasn't so sure. He already lived with one scientist. Perhaps two would have been twice as bad. He couldn't say that to Joe, though.

"Dad doesn't like to talk about Mum much."

Joe smiled at him. "I wish you could have known her, Robbie. Jane was a gifted scientist. She really loved her work." He was chewing fast again. Science was his favourite topic.

Robbie swallowed. It was hard to concentrate on what Joe was saying. His head was buzzing again and he looked around, hoping to find someplace where he could sit down. Joe didn't notice. He was in full flow.

"It's such an amazing feeling, to know you're reshaping the basic building blocks of life, making things that sometimes never existed before. And working with your mother was a real privilege. She was like an artist. Especially with the Hox genes. It took me years to duplicate her work ..."

He broke off and looked at Robbie curiously. "Are you okay? You look really pale."

"I'm fine." But Robbie wasn't fine at all. The insistent pull that had drawn him all the way from the car park to the animal house was fierce now, dragging him forward almost against his will. With a mingled sense of dread and expectation, he pointed to the far end of the building.

"What's down there?"

"Not much." Joe led the way. "We were involved in a project to reintroduce native species into the wild, natural predators, to keep the deer under control. But the focus has changed — now we're concentrating on specifics."

Robbie could tell Joe was quoting someone. From the buzzwords he had heard at home lately when his father was talking on the phone, it was almost certainly Gavin Moir.

In defiance of his growing nausea, he made a determined effort to look interested as he followed Joe down the central walkway towards the rear of the building. They stopped in front of a large cage set against the back wall.

Robbie peered through the wire, watching the animal inside pace restlessly from one side of the small space to the other. It was a cat, but much bigger than a wildcat, the only native Scottish cat he had ever heard of. He stared at its dark brown fur, dotted with lines of darker spots. "Is she a leopard?"

Joe's eyes shifted between Robbie and the cat. A puzzled frown creased his forehead. "How did you know she's female?"

Robbie frowned. He had been asking himself the same question. "Just a wild guess?"

"Well, you're right." Joe tapped gently on the roof of the cage. "Hello, Freya," he said softly.

The cat stopped pacing and moved closer to the mesh. Her whiskers twitched and Robbie saw the ruff of pale fur round her face fluff out like a hood. She was interested in the outdoor smell from his rain-dampened jacket. He looked at the tufted ears, the solid, muscular body and the oddly clubbed tail.

"Not a leopard." Joe confirmed what Robbie had already realized. "Although a lot of people think that, because of the spots. She's a lynx. From Norway. But cats like this used to live all over Europe, including Scotland."

"Why did you bring her here?" Robbie stared at the cat. The cat stared back. There was nothing there, nothing to explain the pressure that was now building up to the point where his head felt as though it might explode.

Joe bristled, feeling accused of something. "We didn't kidnap her, if that's what you mean. Freya got hit by a car. Her hip's pretty much healed now, though. Soon she'll be going back to where she came from. We took her because we were looking for another cat to keep this one company."

With a theatrical flourish, Joe waved an arm in the direction of a neighbouring cage. "Our very own Baldur, born two years ago, right here at the Institute." There was both pride and ownership in his voice.

Hardly able to think, let alone move, Robbie forced himself to turn and look. Shadows shifted at the back of the cage, unfolding into a creature of gold and black. The lynx stretched and yawned, then padded forward, looking up at him intently.

Robbie stared into those ancient, knowing eyes and felt a sudden jolt of recognition, even though he knew he had never seen this animal before. The tugging sensation intensified into a dizzying dislocation, as though his head had come adrift from the rest of his body.

He squeezed his eyes shut, opened them again and blinked, unable to make sense of what he saw. A series of squares floated in front of his eyes. It was mesh. Wire mesh. Beyond the wire he saw a face. There was someone looking down at him — a boy with brown eyes, floppy dark hair and an expression of fixed disbelief. It was the face Robbie saw every morning when he looked in the bathroom mirror.

Annemarie Allan

Breaker

When Tom and Beth move to North Berwick they are faced with a rainy, windswept beach, nothing to do and a whole summer with no friends. Then they meet Professor MacBlain, with his weird and wonderful inventions. Little do they know that he has a secret: not only is he a thief, but he has stolen the one thing that can save the Firth of Forth from environmental catastrophe.

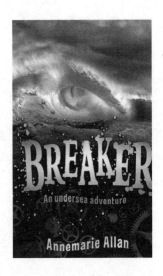